The Protectors Series

Damon

By

Teresa Gabelman

THE PROTECTORS

DAMON

Copyright 2011 Teresa Gabelman

Gabelman, Teresa (2011-11-28).

THE PROTECTORS 'DAMON'.

Paperback Edition.

Editor: Hot Tree Editing

Photo: Denver Photo Pro (Bigstock Photo)

Cover Art: Indie Digital Publishing LLC

Acknowledgements

I would like to thank everyone who has helped me on my journey to fulfill my dream. So to, in no specific order, Ron, Cody, Emma aka Gran, Kelly, Marlene and Beth thank you for putting up with me. You will never know exactly what you have done for me. I cannot put into words the gratitude I have for each and every one of you for helping me along this road....my journey....my dream. Thank you!!!!!

Chapter 1

Nicole Callahan's piece of crap on wheels slid sideways into the wet parking lot. The muffler clanged loudly as she slammed her brakes to stop in front of the old warehouse. Man, she hated to be late and because her face got in the way of someone's fist, she was really running late.

Peering into the review mirror, she groaned. Her eye was already turning a lovely shade of black. Oh well, it wasn't the first black eye she'd ever had and it probably wouldn't be the last. Grabbing her bag out of the backseat, she climbed out and trotted toward the door. Glancing around the parking lot quickly, it looked like she was the last to arrive. With a deep breath, she pushed open the door. "Well, this should be a freakin hoot."

"Good God, Callahan. What happened to your face?" Mitchell Reed yelled as she blew into the room.

"I could ask you the same thing boss" Throwing her bag down, she felt everyone's eyes on her.

"Stop being a smart ass and tell me what happened?" Mitchell stomped toward her. He was a huge man with a permanent scowl as if he was ready to bite your head off any second. Most of the time, in her case, he was ready to do just that.

Grabbing her sweats and t-shirt out of her bag, she headed toward the bathroom.

"My routine check wasn't so routine. It seems Mr. Mullins has an addiction that his new foster child is supplying. I caught him in the act of draining the poor kid. He didn't appreciate the interruption."

"Son of a bitch," Mitch cursed then turned toward the workout area. "What the hell are you stopping for? Get your asses' moving," he yelled sending everyone stumbling over one another.

Nicole came out of the bathroom in sweats and a t-shirt, her long blonde hair pulled into a messy ponytail. "Can you explain again why we're here?" Nicole tossed her clothes onto her bag as she passed it, stopping in front of Mitch.

"Ah...have you seen your face?" Mitch's hands tightened into fists, his scowl fierce. "This is getting more and more dangerous. I can't have you guys out there without training."

"Yeah, I know," Nicole agreed, looking around hating again that she was late. Everyone else was running laps. Her eyes landed on three guys standing in the middle of the running group. "Who are they?"

"They, for the next couple of months, are your instructors."

"Dang, could they be any bigger?" They were huge. The tallest of the group turned to glare at her looking highly annoyed. "They make you look like a midget."

"Yeah, well, guess you better get your ass out there Callahan." Mitch shoved her toward the group of runners, "Looks like they don't like anyone being late."

Nicole stumbled into the group and took off jogging. "About time you got here Callahan. You think you're special or something?" Chad Evans, better known as jackass, complained as he huffed past her.

"I know I am," Nicole snapped, adding under her breath, "jerk."

Nicole caught up with Pam Braxton, who she usually partnered up with on cases. "What happened to you?" Pam huffed, sweat sliding down her face.

"Got caught with my hands down," Nicole grimaced. Running was making her eye throb. "Is this all I've missed so far?"

"Yeah." Wiping sweat off her face with her shirt, Pam kept pace then nodded toward the three men in the middle of the mats, "They just came out and said to start running. God, I think I'm going to die. How in the hell is this going to help with our jobs? I'm not going to be doing any job if I'm dead."

Nicole chuckled as she glanced at the three men. Mitch stood with them talking. She looked away when they all turned to glare at her.

"Okay, everybody stop and take a knee." Mitch's booming voice echoed off the warehouse walls.

"Take a knee? What the hell is he talking about…take a knee?" Pam moaned as they headed toward the men. "If the SOB doesn't let me sit on my well cushioned butt, I'm going to flop over right here on this mat and die. I didn't see him running. Did you?"

Nicole grinned. Pam was a trip. They became fast friends the day they met. Nicole knelt on the mat helping Pam down. Where Nicole was short and curvy, Pam was tall and stick thin.

There were eight employees who worked for Mitch in the Special Family Services Department of Clermont County. Special meaning they worked with vampire and human children. Nicole and Pam were the only women and it had been an uphill battle for both of them. Most of the men, along with Mitch, had accepted them, but Chad and his little followers of merry jackasses did everything in their power to make the ladies lives in the department a living hell. It was just the eight of them standing between innocent children in the county and the ones who would use them for greed. No one else wanted the job. In all honesty, it was too dangerous for most and the small paycheck every two weeks didn't inspire new employees.

"Jesus people," Mitch shook his head in disgust. "Breathe in through the nose out through the mouth. I can't hear myself think with all that huffing you wimps are doing."

Nicole cocked her eyebrow at that. Her breathing was just fine since she ran a minimum of five miles a day.

"Yeah, I know Callahan. You're the shit when it comes to running," Mitch stepped to the side, slightly away from the three men standing behind him.

"Suck up," Chad whispered behind her. Acting like she was fixing her shirt, she flipped him the bird.

Mitch ignored them. "Okay, here it is guys. Ever since the vampire race decided to let us know they were and have been a part of our everyday life, we've been knee deep in funky shit. It's no secret that vampire blood, better known on the streets as Crimson Rush, has hit the Social Service Departments all across the country hard. Human and vampire kids are being sent out to homes and it's our job to make sure the homes we send them to are safe. Humans want to adopt vampire kids and vampires want to adopt human kids. Pretty screwed up if you ask me, but who the hell am I to say what's right or wrong.

"Most of these types of adoptions are legit, but the ones that aren't, is what we're dealing with right now. As you know, some human adopters are using the vampire kids as their very own drug producer, harvesting their blood. And the vampires are turning the human kids to sell for money. It's a cluster fuck of a mess. Your jobs have become more dangerous than they were a year ago. Just take a look at Callahan's face. You may not have had a seriously dangerous situation yet, but it's coming. That's why I have decided to call in the experts to train you how to better protect yourself while doing your job."

Everyone's focus went to the three men. Now that her gaze wouldn't draw attention since everyone was staring, Nicole was instantly aware of how perfect and gorgeous these men were. They all wore the same black workout sweats with black tank tops. Talk about muscles and hard bods. Glancing up, her gaze locked on golden eyes glaring deeply into her baby blues. Shivering, she turned her attention back to Mitch doing her best to keep her focus glued to her boss.

"Before I turn you over to these guys, I want to let you know that this is mandatory. Five nights a week, weekends, and whenever they want you for as long as they want you. Before you open your mouth Callahan, we will work out the details of emergencies like you had tonight as they come up," Mitch glared at her.

Where was all the glaring coming from? "Didn't say a word boss."

"Maybe not out loud, but I know what's in that head of yours before it makes it to your big mouth," Mitch grumbled loudly.

"Impressive," Nicole murmured to Pam, "scary, but impressive." Pam chuckled.

Mitch glared for another few seconds at the women before continuing. "These men have taken time out of their busy schedules to help make you guys safe, so I expect nothing but respect for each of them. This is Duncan Roark, Jared Kincaid and Damon DeMasters. They belong to the Vampire Council, the group of warriors we've been hearing about in the news."

Nicole heard the buzzing of her coworkers behind her as her eyes shot up to the one named Damon. If you haven't heard of the Vampire Council Warriors, then you have either been living under a rock or dead. One year ago, almost to the day, as the vampires made known they were not only in the movies but living among the human race, the VC Warriors were keeping the peace between the two races along with the human Special Forces. Turning humans without special council approval and also consent from the human, was a warrant for death which was carried out by these special warriors.

The blonde vampire, Duncan, stepped up beside Mitch. "We've been working closely with Mitch to see exactly where we can help you carry out your jobs. As we can't be everywhere, and have many rogue vampires running rampant, the children of the two races have fallen between the cracks. The reason the Council has approved us working with you is because they believe that what you do is just as important as what we do." Duncan nodded toward the other two, "We are here to instruct you on how to protect yourselves and will be pairing up with some of you on your jobs to see exactly what you're dealing with. The goal is to prepare you for anything that comes your way."

"Who exactly is pairing up with who?" Pam raised her hand, and then snapped it back down, embarrassment coloring her cheeks. "Nicole and I have the heaviest case load, but some of the others have more dangerous areas."

Mitch stepped in on this question. "Even though they have more dangerous areas, that doesn't really have anything to do with who is breaking the law and using these children. We're going to pair Jared and Damon with you and Callahan since you two have the most cases. Duncan is up in the air right now. The Council has said that if we need more help it will be offered to us, but we are to start out with these guys. Now to get us started, Callahan, why don't you tell us exactly what happened tonight and we can go from there."

Nicole started flicking her thumb nail nervously, an old habit. She hated being in the spotlight. "Ah, well, I did my follow up call this afternoon and talked to Mr. Mullins. He sounded nervous, talking fast, and clearing his throat a lot. I asked how things were going and he assured me everything was fine and that Sam was playing PlayStation. I asked the protocol questions as usual, and even though he answered everything okay, he still sounded nervous and out of breath. I then asked to speak to Sam. He said he wasn't there, that he was playing at a friend's house."

"How old is the boy?" This question came from Damon.

"Eight," Nicole answered without looking directly into those gorgeous golden eyes. "I didn't bring up the fact that he just told me he was playing PlayStation since I knew I was going to do a home visit as soon as I hung up with him. I acted like everything was good, assured him I would talk to him next week and hung up."

"Who did you let know where you were going?" Mitch interrupted.

"I sent Pam a text letting her know. She was already on a scheduled home visit."

"What's the difference?" This again from Damon.

"A scheduled visit is usually less dangerous, as the foster parents know we're coming. We schedule visits up to three months, six months and up to a year depending upon the case. The home visits not scheduled are the most dangerous. Even before Crimson Rush hit the streets, it was more dangerous to do an unscheduled visit. Many of us would find that the foster parents were not who we thought they were." God, the things she had found in those homes kept her awake at night.

"Go on," Damon crossed his arms nodding at Nicole.

"When I got to the house, I sat for a few minutes in the car across the street watching the house to see if anything seemed off. Then I got out and knocked on the door. It wasn't closed all the way, and opened a little when I knocked. I could hear Sam crying. Again I called out, and when no one answered, I hit 911 on my phone and went inside."

Everyone's eyes were on her and she hated having to repeat what she saw. The anger and horror she felt earlier consumed her again at the memory of it. Everyone waited for her to continue.

"The crying seemed to be coming from downstairs, so I headed in that direction, found the door leading to the basement and the crying got louder."

"Please tell me you didn't go down in the basement without backup Callahan," Mitch rubbed his eyes knowing damn good and well that was exactly what she was telling them.

"He was terrified Mitch. What was I supposed to do, just stand there and listen to him scream and cry?" Nicole shook her head. "No way. Not happening."

"You're just damn lucky that black eye is the only thing that happened to you tonight." Mitch nodded for her to continue.

"I headed down the stairs and saw Mr. Mullins leaning over

something. Looking around, I saw an IV stand lying sideways on a long table with a bag of blood hanging from it. At that point, Mr. Mullins had moved and I saw Sam strapped to a chair with IV tubing coming out of one arm. Mr. Mullins was working on a second bag of Sam's blood." Her stomach twisted at the memory. "Not thinking, I headed toward Sam wanting to yank the tube out of his arm, and I guess I surprised Mr. Mullins. He turned and backhanded me."

"I need a full report on this first thing in the morning," Mitch told her, shaking his head in disgust.

Nicole nodded as she continued, "After he hit me, I heard someone run up the stairs. I didn't see who it was, but there was money scattered at the bottom of the steps and a busted bag of what I assume was Sam's blood. By then, the police were there and had Mr. Mullins under control and Sam was being taken care of by the paramedics." Glancing over, she saw Damon's scowl.

"Do you have any idea what kind of danger you put yourself in?" Damon demanded, looking at the small blonde woman who had the biggest blue eyes he'd ever seen. The bruising under one of those lovely eyes had his blood raging. Ever since she had walked through the door, he had an overwhelming urge to protect her, and that confused the hell out of him, making him growl his question at her.

"Yeah, I do, but at the time my only concern was for Sam," she scowled back. "I have never, and I hope I never again, see what I saw tonight. For a child, vampire or human, to go through something like this is uncalled for, and I'll do everything in my power to see that Mr. Mullins is never allowed to be near a child again."

"I still think you are taking grave risks that you are ill equipped to take, human," Damon scowled, his voice a low deep rumble of authority.

"Yeah, well, it wasn't you who put that child in the hands of a monster, vamp," Nicole shot back. If he thought to scare her with the big bad vampire warrior thing he had going on, he was sadly mistaken. Backing down wasn't an option when it came to her job.

"Ah....okay," Duncan stepped in not liking where this was heading. "Everybody partner up."

Mitch glared a warning at Nicole, who just shrugged and mouthed, "He started it." Taking a quick peek at the warrior, she noticed his smug grin. Oh yeah, this was going to be a problem.

Chapter 2

Nicole came into the office early the next morning to write her report. She should have done it the previous night since she hadn't slept a wink. Between thinking of Damon and the nightmare of what happened to Sam, her brain wouldn't stop working. Tossing the pen across the desk, she rubbed her eyes wishing the images of Sam strapped to that chair with silver chains and the tube running out of his arm would fade, but she knew they wouldn't.

Sam had been taken off the streets by the Cincinnati police a month ago and turned over to their care. Mitch had sent her to the hospital where he was being looked over. If anyone would have told her two years ago that she would have to place an 8 year old vampire in a foster home, she would have called them crazy. Now they had more vampire children to find homes for than human children. Of course vampires could not have children, but human children were being turned to supply the thirst for the Crimson Rush that had taken over the drug market. Some days she just wanted to head to the mountains somewhere and disappear. God, it was heartbreaking and truly scary. It was a new world they lived in with different rules, one she was hoping she could live in without going insane.

Pam peeked her head through the doorway, "Mitch is yelling for you."

"What's new?" Taking her hand away from her eyes she grabbed her report and got up. "Are you sore?"

"Are you kidding me?" Pam moaned. "It took me five minutes to sit down on the toilet this morning, my butt is so sore. It was pretty comical."

Nicole laughed, "Yeah, it took me a while to get moving."

"Wonder if one of those warriors would rub my bum to make it feel better?" Pam snickered, her face turning red. "I wanted to die when we had to partner up with them last night. Talk about a work out."

"I guess they wanted to make sure we were getting the moves right since we are just women folk." She didn't want to let on to Pam how much having Damon's hands on her affected her. Every time he grabbed her in a hold, it felt like a sizzle of electricity coursing through her body. She'd never felt anything like it before and the truth was she kinda liked it. "Ah, did you feel, I don't know, something weird when Jared was working with you?"

They headed down the hall towards Mitch's office. "You mean did I want to jump his bones?" Pam sighed dramatically. "Well, hell yeah."

"I'm waiting for that report Callahan," Mitch's booming shout bounced down the hall toward them.

Rolling her eyes, she stepped into his office tossing him the report. "Patience is a virtue Mitch."

"Yeah, well, I wouldn't know virtue if it bit me on the ass and to hell with patience," Mitch grunted, thumbing through the report. "Damon and Jared have been waiting for you both. I'm about ready to put them on the payroll since they're the only ones who seem to be able to tell time."

Nicole glanced at the clock. "It's only three after. Most places give their employees a seven minute window." She purposely ignored the two men she figured were taking up the chairs behind her. She wasn't ready to face the large warriors yet, one in particular. She hadn't thought they would be here this early.

Mitch slammed the report down to glare at her. "I'm not in the mood for your smart mouth remarks Callahan. We have a full schedule today and you all need to train tonight so getcha asses in gear. Pam, you and Jared are pairing up today and Damon is going with you Callahan."

Nicole heard the two men behind her stand. "No prob boss." She turned to walk out the door then stopped, "Oh, by the way, you owe the jar a dollar."

Mitch looked up from his desk, his eyes narrowed. "I didn't say the f-word."

"No, not today, but you did last night." Nicole glanced over at the jar that was packed full of dollar bills, mostly Mitch's hard earned money. "I'm proud of ya boss. Only one, that's quite an improvement."

Mitch stood digging into his pocket, then placed another dollar in the jar marked 'F-WORD' in big bold letters. They actually kept it in his office since he contributed to the jar more than anyone. "If you want a seven minute window for your late ass Callahan, be my guest to find another place to work," Mitch threw out behind her.

"You know you love me boss." Nicole chuckled. "Who else is going to keep you on your toes?"

"God help me," Mitch groaned before slamming his door shut.

Jared chuckled as the four made their way down the hall, "What was that all about?"

"Since we work with children so much, we have to watch our language. So Nicole made the 'F-WORD' jar. She uses the money at the end of the year to help with a Christmas party for the kids," Pam chuckled. "Mitch is the worst offender of the f-word and Nicole calls him on it every time."

"Is it just that word or others along with it?" Jared's eyes crinkled with humor.

"Just the f-word," Pam snickered. "Everyone has to eat and pay bills. Nicole tried for them all, but everyone revolted because their paychecks were disappearing into the jar."

"Hey, it's not my fault everyone around here has a potty mouth," Nicole grumbled.

They stopped in front of Nicole's office. Jared dug into his wallet,

"Guess since we're going to be helping, I need to watch my mouth." Jared handed Nicole a twenty. "That should do it until I can get control of my favorite word."

Smiling, Nicole nodded, "Yeah, cause vampire warrior or not, I will call you on it."

"She's ruthless when it comes to making money for the kids," Pam chuckled. "Everyone who comes in on a regular basis is warned about it because we do have kids in here sometimes. She got the UPS guy last week."

"I'm not ruthless," Nicole turned to head into her office, "I'm determined."

Pam looked up at Damon, "What about you? You tossing in now or waiting until she catches you?"

"I have more control than Jared." Damon grinned at Jared's eye roll.

Jared snorted, "Yeah, right. I bet you've said it at least twenty times this morning already."

"Didn't have a reason not to," Damon looked down at Nicole and winked. "Now I do."

"You'll slip," Jared gave a confident nod.

"Yeah, well, if he does, I'll call him on it too," Nicole warned. She was a little shocked that these rough and tough warriors would play along.

"You guys be careful out there," Pam called out as she and Jared continued down the hall.

"Same to you," Nicole responded as she walked into her office. Sitting down, she glanced up to see Damon standing in her door, his broad shoulders blocking any thought of a quick exit. Talk about claustrophobic. "Oh, I forgot I had to invite you in since you're a vamp and all."

Damon couldn't help but grin revealing straight white teeth and flashing some fang. "Ah, that's a vamp myth, human." With one step, he filled her small office and took a seat in front of her desk. "And this isn't your home."

"Could have fooled me," Snorting, she marked an envelope 'Jared's f-word money' and slipped the twenty in. "Might as well call this place home sweet home since I'm here more often than not."

"Better watch out, if Mitch hears you talking like that, he might take rent out of your check," his eyes twinkled. He really liked her sense of humor. Most women tried too hard to impress him into their beds and that bored him almost before they even began.

Nicole laughed, liking this side of the warrior. She felt more at ease with him. Humor always made her comfortable. "I wouldn't put it past the man that's for sure. Anything to make my life miserable."

"I'd say the same about you." Damon leaned back in the chair smiling at her, "You seem to like making his life miserable."

"Interesting," Nicole countered with a smile of her own, "not miserable. He seriously wouldn't know what to do without me. I was sick a couple of months ago and was out for one day. He called me every hour."

Damon nodded, and then looked around her cluttered office. Case files were scattered everywhere. "So would he or anyone else know your filing system? I'm sure even Mitch would splurge for a filing cabinet."

"Only I know my extensive and complicated filing system. I know it looks like a mess, but if anyone needed anything, I could pull it in a minute flat. File cabinets take up space."

Again he grinned and man, did that lopsided curve of those full lips make him sexy as hell. "So you have no problem with me heading out to jobs with you?"

Trying not to squirm under his scrutiny, she shuffled the case files around her desk trying to look busy. "No. Why would you ask that?"

"You just don't seem like the kind of woman who wants a man following her every move." Relaxing more, he leaned back crossing his heavily muscled arms across his massive chest.

Stopping herself from wiping her mouth to check for drool, she eyed him. "Listen, I care for these kids. I know I shouldn't care as much as I do and Mitch gets on me for getting too involved, but I can't help it. Not one of these kids have asked for what is happening to them, so anything you and your fellow buddies can do to help, you'll get no problems from me. I do know that I get in over my head sometimes, and I don't think, but when I see a kid in pain or scared, all I can think about is getting them out of the situation."

"Do all of you feel the same about this job?" The only thing that moved was his lips as he asked the question. His eyes, so golden, probed so deeply into hers, it was truly unsettling.

"I really can't answer for them." She glanced away, "I do know Mitch wouldn't keep anyone on that didn't do their job and do it well."

"What about Chad Evans?"

She shrugged one shoulder, "What about him? He does his job just like the rest of us."

"But you don't like him." It wasn't a question. "He doesn't like you." That was fact.

"Well, there you go," Nicole snorted. "We don't really work together except for meetings and now working out with you guys, so it really isn't a problem."

16

"But you don't trust him." Again statement rather than question.

Blue eyes stared into gold. "How would you know something like that? Can you read my mind, vamp? Cause if you can, it's awfully scary in there." She tapped her temple with her pen.

He studied her closely, his gaze intense before answering. "No, I can't read yours."

Shocked, she dropped her pen. "But you can read others?"

"Yes."

"Oh, well, ah, is that good or bad?" she chuckled, nerves cramping her stomach. God, no way did she want this hot vampire lurking in her mind, so it was very good on her end.

"I don't know yet." He frowned. "It's never happened before."

"You mean you've never not been able to read someone's mind?" Wow, that would be kind of cool to read people's mind. Then again thinking of Mitch, she probably wouldn't want to know what he really thought of her most of the time.

"No, you're the first human I haven't been able to read." He did look quite puzzled by this whole idea of not being able to read her. "But you're happy about the fact that I can't."

"You bet I am." Standing, she shoved her case files into her work bag, "Who wants someone poking around into your deepest thoughts, your private thoughts?"

He stood and opened the door for her. "It saves time," his voice rumbled close to her as she passed him on the way out. "You don't have to ask questions."

"Well...there is that," Nicole gave a nervous chuckle as she breezed past him, not wanting him to see how his closeness affected her. Man this was going to be a long day.

After stopping at the hospital to check on Sam, who had been happily eating ice cream, they had gone to the homes that Nicole had scheduled visits. Everything had gone well and everyone seemed to be happy with no problems. It has been a rare day. They were now heading back to the office.

"You love this job don't you?" Damon glanced at her before turning his attention back to the road. He had insisted on driving after seeing her car. He had advised her that he would not step foot in the piece of crap she called a car. Nicole had to agree with him. It was a piece of crap and she would talk to Mitch first thing in the morning about a raise or company vehicle. Yeah...like that was going to happen.

"Yeah, I do," she nodded then touched her black eye. "Does have its downfalls I guess, but I wouldn't want to be doing anything else. I just wish there was more I could do."

"Like what? It seems like you are doing all that you can."

"No, not really. There's a war out there with this blood addiction stuff that needs to be stopped. I just wish I could have seen who else was in that basement yesterday. It could be a clue to whoever is behind all of this."

"You are not to do anything about that," Damon's grip on the steering wheel tightened, his voice hard. His alpha male protective instincts for this woman kicked into high gear.

"Listen, I don't care if you come along and all that, but don't think you can tell me what to do because I'll do whatever the hell I want to do," Nicole shot right back.

"Listen to me Nicole. We have been working this for a long time and this is something that is too dangerous to get involved in," Damon's voice rumbled in warning.

"What do you mean get involved in?" she huffed turning completely in her seat to face him noting that his eyes were getting darker. "I am involved up to my eyeballs in this stuff. I want it stopped before more children get hurt."

"And you don't think we want it stopped? We have leads we are working on every day and the ones involved would rather kill you first and ask questions later." His eyes seemed to go black as night as he slid a sideways glare at her.

"I know, but I'm on the inside, so to speak. I hear a lot of stuff and could help out. Plus, you guys are teaching us how to protect ourselves."

"No!" Damon growled. "Dammit Nicole, stay out of it. You don't have a clue what you're getting yourself into." He pulled into an empty parking space in front of her office.

Nicole had the door opened before he even stopped, "Yeah...whatever." She leaped out of the car slamming the door.

"Damn!" Damon slammed his hands on the steering barely catching himself from saying the f-word. Shaking his head in disbelief, he couldn't help the disgusted chuckle that escaped his lips. "After hundreds of years one small blonde woman has me calling fuck the f-word. Yeah...some badass warrior I am." He was truly screwed. Watching to make sure she made it to her car, he backed out and headed to the warehouse.

***

Nicole could feel Damon glaring hotly at her as she ran her laps to warm up. She had lost her temper earlier and felt bad about it. She knew he was here to help them and they desperately needed these warrior's help. She just couldn't help but react to him. Noticing he was standing alone, she stopped in front of him. "Listen, I'm sorry about earlier. I tend to get a little defensive about my job. I'm not stupid and I know we need your help. It's just I want to do everything I can to stop this."

Damon nodded, his eyes back to their golden stage. "I understand your passion for what you do, but the deeper you involve yourself, the more danger you place yourself in. You can't help anyone if you get yourself killed."

"I have a lot of contacts." Nicole glanced over her shoulder to see if anyone was listening. "I hear a lot, so if I hear anything I think will help, I'll let you know and you can check it out. Does that sound fair?"

"As long as it doesn't put you in danger, then I'll agree." He nodded toward the middle of the mat, "Come on, you need to work on your ground fighting skills."

Nicole tried not to stick her tongue out as he passed her. "Well, alrighty then," she snorted, and followed him trying not to look at the way his workout pants clung to his tight butt.

Damon stopped in the middle of the mat and turned toward her, "Lay down and spread your legs."

Nicole stopped suddenly, her eyes shooting from his ass to his face. "Ah, most guys buy me a drink first." At his raised eyebrow, Nicole snorted, "Okay. Sorry. Just a joke. You know you can probably buy a sense of humor on Craigslist."

"There's nothing wrong with my sense of humor." Once she was on the ground, he knelt between her legs. "I just didn't find that funny."

Nicole rolled her eyes then gasped when he grabbed both her wrists and held them above her head with one hand. "Hey!"

He leaned over her slightly putting some of his weight on her keeping her immobile. "Most confrontations you are going to face as a woman are going to end in this position. We have been showing you how not to end up here, but chances are you will end up here." His eyes drilled into hers, his breath tickling her face. "I want you to try to get away from me however you think you can. Don't worry about hurting me."

"After that 'not funny' remark, no worries there," Nicole snorted and then started bucking, twisting and turning, but nothing happened except her out of breath gasping. Then an idea popped in her head. "Ow. Ow. Ow. Cramp. Major freakin cramp."

Damon rolled off her concerned, "Where?"

Seeing her chance, she jumped on his back and got him in a choke hold they had been shown last night. "Ah ha. Gotcha." Before she knew what was happening, she was flipped over his head and back in the same position she was in before her sneak attack.

"Nice try human, but your attacker isn't going to care if you have a cramp so that didn't count."

"Okay, you got me." Nicole couldn't help but notice how damn gorgeous he was when he smiled, plus he smelled amazing. Then she noticed something else. "Why do your eyes change colors? I've seen them black, dark brown and then light gold."

"I'm about ready to tear your throat out with my fangs and you want to know about my eye color?" Eyebrow cocked, his lips did the sexy half smile thing, "Is this another sneak attack?"

"Maybe." She felt stupid asking now, but she really wanted to know. "I mean, it seems to me it goes with your moods, so wouldn't that maybe help us when dealing with another vampire."

Damon seemed surprised, "You're correct. It does have to do with my... I guess you could say *moods*. Black is usually when I'm angry or hungry." He flashed a fang at her. "The lighter they get, I guess, the lighter the mood and less hungry."

Okay, the fang flashing was a total turn on. Mentally smacking herself, she got back on track. "Is that just you or all of your kind?"

"All of us. I've noticed it before, but never determine moods by it since I can read vampires and humans without seeing their eyes." He grinned leaning closer to her their noses almost touching, "What color are they now?"

Nicole swallowed hard, "Ah, light."

"Guess that's a good thing for you, human," he teased then backed off slightly.

Jared walked by and stopped, "Are you going to lay on her all night talking or are you going to teach her something?"

"Fuck you, Jared," Damon growled without taking his eyes off her. "Let the others know about our eye color changes. The little human here is quite observant, and it could help them gauge their situation in the future."

"Nice," he nodded down at Nicole. "Didn't think about that."

"Yeah, well even *us* lowly humans have some smarts," Nicole rolled her eyes. "Now how about telling me how to get this huge vamp off me."

After working for a half an hour to escape from different ground positions, everyone was heading to the showers. Pam and Nicole grabbed their bags and were leaving the workout floor when Chad stepped in front of them.

"I hope you don't think you're going to get brownie points screwing that vampire Callahan," Chad snickered along with his follower's. "I mean damn, how long was he between them legs of yours tonight?"

Pam grabbed Nicole's arm. "Come on Nicole," Pam pulled her, "he isn't worth it."

Knowing she was right, Nicole kept tight control on her tongue and tried to walk around him, but he wasn't about to let it go. "It's sad really." He got in her face. "You making the rest of us look bad by acting like a slut. If that's the case, I want to work on the ground stuff with you so I can get between them legs."

Before Nicole had a chance to shoot off at the mouth, Chad was picked up and shoved halfway across the room. Jared and Duncan both grabbed Damon holding him back. Shoving them both off, Damon marched toward Chad who was just picking himself up off the mat.

Nicole took off after him. "Damon no!" Nicole jumped in front of him putting her hand on his chest. "Don't. He's not worth it and I don't care what he says. He always says stupid stuff. Kind of the norm. Just ask Pam." Nicole tried to make light of the situation just to head off a killing.

"What the hell's going on?" Mitch boomed as he came from the showers. "Callahan what did you do this time?"

Nicole rolled her eyes ignoring her boss, "Seriously, vamp. He's not worth it." Finally his eyes left Chad and lowered to hers. "Uh-oh. You're either really hungry or level 10 pissed cause your eyes are blacker than a...ah...well, I don't know what, but they are pretty freakin black."

His lips twitched before his eyes left hers and zeroed in on Chad. "Apologize now." It was a demand, not a suggestion.

Everyone held their breath, well everyone but the vampires in the room, waiting to see exactly how smart or stupid Chad was. "For what?" Chad, newly nicknamed stupid ass, looked to Nicole. "I'm just stating the truth."

"I asked a question people," Mitch walked between Chad, Nicole and Damon probably saving Chad's life.

"He is not welcome here again until he apologizes to Nicole," Damon growled, his black piercing eyes pinning Chad to the spot. "I will not tolerate a male, human or vampire, who disrespects a woman." Especially this woman his actions roared.

Mitch turned toward Chad demanding to know what the hell was going on as Jared and Duncan filled him in. With one last growl directed toward Chad, Damon lowered his eyes once again to Nicole and then to her hand still on his chest.

Pulling her hand quickly away, she flushed. "Thank you." Nicole lowered her eyes feeling shy. What the hell, she didn't have a shy bone in her body, but she had never had anyone, especially a fine piece of male, stand up for her like that. "But like I said, he isn't worth it, so don't worry about him. His words can't hurt me."

"You're not a very good liar, Nicole Callahan." He had seen the hurt flash in her eyes briefly at the bastard's words, and it had sent him over the edge. Luckily, Jared and Duncan had been here or he probably would have killed the son of a bitch. Something about this small human brought out every protective instinct he possessed.

Chad walked up with Mitch closely behind him. "Sorry Nicole," Chad spat throwing her a glare oozing with hate. Ignoring Damon's sneer, he roughly grabbed his bag before slamming out the door.

Damon started to follow him. Nicole knew she had to stop him from killing Chad. "You owe me a dollar vamp."

Caught by surprise, Damon stopped to look down at her, "What?"

"You told Jared to shut the f-up." Nicole gave him a mock frown, "So you owe me a dollar."

Jared burst out laughing, the mood in the room turning much lighter. "She got you bro," Jared chuckled.

Damon finally smiled, but his eyes remained black as midnight. "You can't forgive me for one slip."

"Nope." Nicole picked up her bag, "Sorry vamp. I'll give ya until tomorrow to pay up."

"Ruthless..." Pam smirked shaking her head.

Seeing Mitch scowling at her, Nicole threw her hands in the air. "It wasn't me this time. I have witnesses." She didn't wait for a response. "I'm heading out. See you tomorrow." Waving to Pam she hurried out the door Chad just slammed through.

"Sorry about that guys. I'll talk to them both and make sure that doesn't happen again," Mitch cursed, his hair sticking up from running his hand through it repeatedly. "I don't know what the hell is going on between those two, but they can't be in the same room without something happening."

Nicole headed to her car feeling tears burning the back of her eyes, but held them back. Blindly, she searched for her keys. "I don't know why I lock this piece of crap," she mumbled to herself tossing her gym bag on the hood and rummaging through until she found them. Grabbing her bag, she unlocked her door throwing her bag in harder than necessary. Falling in behind the wheel with a huff, she turned the key, and with a puff of smoke from the tailpipe, it started.

Eyes hidden in the dark moonless night followed her as she zipped out of the parking lot. The dark figure lifted his head slowly sniffing the air. "Mmm, sweet." A sinister smile shaped the man's lips, as the smile spread sharp fangs gleamed, "Perfect."

Chapter 3

Nicole and Pam met up at Club Zero. It was Friday night and they both needed to drown in a beer or two. It was unwind time.

"How's it going with you and Kenny?" Nicole asked over the thumping music. Club Zero was packed for a Friday night. They sat toward the back, away from the dance floor where the crowd merged into one solid mass of bumping and grinding bodies. It was quieter in the back; well at least they didn't have to yell to hear one another. Not even the bathroom stalls were quiet at the dance club.

"Okay I guess," Pam shrugged, before her pink coated lips spread into a grin. "He doesn't like the fact that we're working with vampires. He threw a fit when he found out. I told him that it was safer for us in the long run since we're dealing with a lot of weird stuff now, but he still freaked. Can you imagine what he'll do once he sees the guys we're working with?"

Nicole nodded in agreement tipping her beer. She knew Pam had the hots for Jared. Damn, who wouldn't? The three vampires they were working with looked like they belonged on a magazine cover or romance novel. Kind of sucked hanging around with dudes who had better looking hair than yours. "Yeah, well, he needs to get over it. I mean it's not like we are going to jump their bones and have mad sex while on the job."

"Ha! Speak for yourself," Pam snorted. "Damon is the hottest thing on two legs and you damn well know it."

Nicole shrugged, glancing out over the dance floor as if the conversation bored her to tears. "He's okay I guess. Probably knows how hot he is and plays it to his full advantage on poor unsuspecting females."

"You are such a liar, Nicole," Pam shook her head. "I see you sneaking looks at him during workouts."

"Shut up Pam," Nicole chuckled at her friend. "I don't sneak looks at him. I'm probably trying to slack and just making sure I'm not getting busted."

"Yeah. Yeah. Yeah," Pam rolled her eyes. "Come on. I need to work this soreness out and I love this song." Pam emptied her beer in one gulp then grabbed Nicole before she could say no.

Damon and Jared walked into the smoke filled club; music blaring, bodies smashed together and the smells of sweat and sex hung heavy in the air, making their highly sensitive sense of smell go into overdrive.

"Do you want to split up?" Jared grinned with a wink at the little red head who rubbed her barely clothed body against his as she brushed past him. Licking her lush red painted lips with invitation, she moved slowly away, her hips swaying seductively. "Or do you want me to follow that red head and see exactly what she can do with those lips?"

Damon ignored him as he scanned the area. They had been told that Jamison would be here tonight. He was an assassin who'd take out his own mother, not because of money, but because he got off on it. The news on the street was that he had a new target, and someone high up in the blood trafficking business, had given the kill order. The kill was to be made tonight. Their informant was hardly ever wrong, so Damon was ready for anything tonight. They had been hunting this son of bitch for too long. Running his hands through his black hair, Damon pulled it into a ponytail and tied it with a leather strip. Yeah too long, and tonight the bastard was going down. They would keep him alive to get information out of him, but that didn't mean they couldn't have a little fun first.

"Get your head out of your ass and get focused." Damon spotted the vampire at the edge of the dance floor. "We need to do this with as little notice as possible." Even though they had the authority of the government, they still had to work within the guidelines of the law, just like the human police. It wasn't the same as before the vampires were outed. 'Find the bad vamp...kill the bad vamp' was their motto, and still was when no witnesses were around.

Jared spotted him and nodded, all memory of the red head gone. Jared may be a goof and loved the ladies, but he took his job seriously and was damn good at it. Just an inch shy of Damon's six-three, Jared sided up next to his comrade ready to get the job done. "Let's get the bastard."

"Wait a minute," Damon grabbed his arm. "Unless he makes a sudden move, let's try to see who the target is. I'll keep my eyes on him and you see if you can tell who it is." Damon knew the minute Jamison found his target, the vamp's body language shifted. Damon knew they couldn't wait any longer.

"Now!" Damon took off one way while Jared took off another. Not knowing what was coming his way, Jamison headed toward his target. The humans in the club had no clue what was about to go down, but the vampires did and scattered quickly out of the way.

As soon as the song ended, Pam and Nicole headed off the dance floor as all hell broke loose. Hearing an inhuman roar behind them, Nicole turned to see a huge man barreling his way toward them pushing and throwing people out of his way as if they weighed no more than dolls. Knowing for certain she and Pam were next, instinct took over. With no thought to herself, she pushed Pam out of the way at the same time she felt herself being grabbed in a bone bruising grip. Before she could be thrown like the other unfortunate club goers, he was tackled to the ground. Unfortunately, she was tackled with him.

Nicole knew she was going to die. She had a spilt second of grim amusement at the knowledge that it would be in the middle of a screaming crowd on a sticky dance floor. Spots danced across her vision, as the weight of two bodies forced all air out of her lungs and through her mouth in a short scream. The saddest part was her last vision on earth was going to be of black eyes rimmed with red, and saliva drooling fangs of the ugliest vampire she'd ever seen, his fangs snapping trying to rip out her throat.

Damon straddled Jamison's back, grabbing him by the hair trying to yank him off the human woman. He almost lost his hold when he saw Nicole laying still and pale on the floor, her honey-colored hair spread out with a hint of blood near the crown. "Jared!" he roared over the crowd's screams. As Jared ran up, he stopped cold seeing Pam and Nicole. "Take this son of a bitch." Damon tossed Jamison not taking his eyes off Nicole.

Pam had raced up leaning over Nicole. "Oh my God," she panicked. "Nicole! Is she dead?"

"Move," Damon demanded more calmly than he felt, pushing Pam away carefully. Tuning everyone out, he felt overwhelming relief hearing a steady heartbeat coming from Nicole's still body. Leaning down, he touched her cheek, "Nicole honey. Wake up."

"I'm a nurse. Let me through," A woman pushed her way through the crowd. Kneeling down, she grabbed Nicole's wrist. "What's her name?"

"Nicole." Damon hadn't moved. Couldn't move. His eyes were riveted on Nicole's pale, still face. He felt an overwhelming urge to push the woman away, but knew she was only trying to help. His hands shook as he picked up Nicole's cold hand, needing to touch her.

Carefully, the woman crooked a hand under Nicole's neck and lifted her head slowly to check where the blood seemed to be coming from. It wasn't a lot of blood, but it was enough to have the vampires who stuck around lick their lips in frenzied anticipation. Damon was no exception.

Pam watched as a few vampires inched their way toward Nicole with an excited hungry glow in their black eyes. With a leap, she shielded Nicole's body. "Oh my God," Pam freaked. "Get away from her!"

Damon's head snapped at Pam's scream. Seeing the hungry vampires advancing with predatory grace, Damon put his body between them and Nicole without hesitation. "The first motherfucker who even looks thirsty will die. You got me?" Damon eyed everyone, vampire or not. Most vampires had their shit together and didn't blood lust at the sight of human blood, the legal blood banks helped, but some blood called out to them, and Nicole's was a spicy warm scent and even had his mouth watering. All of them, but one, turned to leave the scene. "You got a death wish, pal?" Damon sneered. With one last longing glance at Nicole's blood, the vampire turned and walked away.

Nicole slowly opened her eyes focusing them on Pam who sat beside her, head bent crying. "Hey," she moaned, her hand automatically flying to her head. "Did you get the make and model of that vampire?"

"Nicole?" Pam scrambled to her knees. "Oh God, are you okay?"

"Do you know where you are?" A woman who Nicole didn't know leaned over her using her thumb and index finger to open one eye then the other.

"Yeah," Nicole licked her dry lips. "I'm lying on the dirty dance floor of Club Zero."

"She may have a concussion, but I don't think a bad one. Her pupils look good and the blood on the back of her head looks more like a scrape, nothing serious," she told Pam before placing her hand under Nicole's upper back. "Can you sit up?"

With the woman and Pam's help, she sat up. A wave of dizziness hit making everything around her spin, and sending a jolt of queasiness to her stomach. Snapping her eyes shut, she swallowed hard. "Wow, head rush. Give me a minute." Once it passed, she opened her eyes slowly to see Damon's gorgeous face in front of her, his black eyes peering into hers. "Hey, what are you doing here?"

"How are you feeling?" he answered her question with a question. She looked pale as hell to him and her eyes seemed a little unfocused. "Are you sure she's alright?" he asked the off duty nurse.

"I think she'll be fine," the woman smiled. "She just had three hundred pounds of male land on top of her, so I think she deserves a minute or two to shake that off. It probably knocked the wind right out of her more than anything."

Slowly turning her head toward the woman, Nicole frowned. "I'm sorry, but who are you?"

The woman chuckled, "I'm Debbie and I watched you get tackled by the man that was escorted out of here, along with this huge fellow. Being a nurse, I figured I'd see if I could help out." Debbie stood brushing off her pants. "It might not be a bad idea to have her checked out at the hospital, but I really think she'll be okay as long as she isn't left alone tonight. Also, if you begin to feel nauseous, start vomiting or have a severe headache, like you want to chop your own head off, you need to get to the emergency room right away."

"Thank you," Damon nodded as he stood, not taking his eyes off Nicole.

"You're welcome," the woman replied, and blushed clearly noticing just how hot Damon was. "Ah, well, you take care and stay out of the way of anymore running males," she told Nicole. Then with one last look at Damon, she walked away.

Nicole snorted, "No problem there and thanks."

Jared ran in as soon as Debbie walked away. "Good God Nicole, are you okay?" Jared knelt down. "I saw you take that hit."

"Yeah, I'm okay," she replied tentatively, unsure if she really was or not; she'd yet to try to stand up.

"If we ever play football, you're on my team," Jared chuckled shaking his head amazed. "Damn, woman."

"Unfortunately, I think I would be a one hit player," she grinned. Putting her hands down, she tried to push herself to her knees. Once there, she waited to see if the dizziness would make another appearance. When it didn't, she put one foot on the floor and tried to stand. Her body protested and her eyes closed as pain shot up her back. Easing herself back down, she moaned, "Maybe I'll just stay here tonight. I don't really mind the stickiness and smell."

Damon was there in a flash picking her up and carefully setting her onto her feet without letting go. "Go slow, honey." He watched her carefully.

Jared stepped back looking at Damon in shock, as did Pam. Jared looked at Pam with raised eyebrows clearly asking a silent, 'Did he just call her honey?' Pam's eyebrows raised in answer.

Nicole let Damon lead her to a bar stool. Once seated, she took a deep breath and winced at the sharp pain throbbing in her ribs. Grabbing her side, she bent slightly to see if that would ease the pain. "Who was that guy?"

Damon watched her closely, ready to catch her if she started to fall. "Are you sure you're okay?"

"Yeah, I'm sure. Just working the kinks out" Nicole frowned. "Now would you please stop answering my questions with questions. What's going on?"

"What the hell are you doing here Nicole?" Damon frowned hearing how harsh he sounded, but dammit, seeing her like this was killing him and he didn't know why. He hardly knew the woman and yet her pain was his pain. And it pissed him off that he had been the cause of her pain.

"I was having a beer and dancing with Pam. We come here to unwind sometimes on Fridays." Nicole couldn't take her eyes off his face. He was so handsome. His eyes were getting lighter, but still hinted at the blackness she seen earlier. His features were strong and harsh with his midnight black hair framing his high cheekbones and square chin. "What are you doing here?"

Jared sauntered up to Damon and Nicole ignoring the tension hovering between them. "That guy that landed on you was an assassin looking to take out a target. We were here to stop him."

"Are you serious?" Nicole's mouth dropped open as she absorbed Jared's revelation. She looked at Pam in horror before turning back to

32

Jared, "Who was he after? Did you find out?"

Jared shook his head, "We have no idea. Before we could figure it out, he made his move, so we had to make ours. We think he was hired by a key player higher up in the..."

Damon slapped Jared in the chest and pushed him back. "I think you need to go and make sure everything is getting taken care of."

"Duncan has already taken him to headquarters." Jared allowed Damon to push him toward the door. "What the hell is your problem?"

"Your mouth," Damon growled. "Go on, I'll be there later."

Jared eyed him and looked over Damon's shoulder at Nicole and Pam. "I'll see you two tomorrow," he told the women. With one last WTF look at Damon, Jared turned and left.

Damon walked back to the two women. "Come on." He took Nicole's elbow, "Let's get you checked out and then home."

"I'm fine. Just get me home," Nicole straightened up slowly.

"I think you should get checked out, Nicole," Pam grabbed their stuff and followed them out.

"I have to feed Ren and Stimpy." Nicole really didn't want to go to the hospital. Hospitals gave her the creeps and she didn't want them to keep her. "I'll be fine."

"Can you stay with her tonight?" Damon asked Pam. "And who the hell are Ren and Stimpy?"

"They're her turtles," Pam chuckled. "Of course I will. I'll just swing by my place and pick up a few things."

"I'll get her home and wait until you get there." Damon slipped his

33

arm around Nicole when she wobbled a little.

"I'm right here guys," Nicole grumbled. "Stop talking about me like I'm not."

"Will you let someone take care of you for once?" Damon scolded gently. Opening the car door, he helped her in. He watched to make sure Pam made it to her car okay before getting in the driver seat. Man, his nerves were shot to hell.

The purr of Damon's sleek Mustang GT was the only thing that broke the silence. Nicole kept her head away from the seat not wanting to get blood on the leather interior. Sneaking a look, the dashboard lights shadowed Damon's smooth chiseled face, his eyes straight ahead as he maneuvered the downtown streets of Cincinnati. His black hair lay against his shoulders in an uneven cut and was pulled away from his face by the numerous sweeps of his hand through his long stands. He was handsome in a way that was hard and masculine, not GQ pretty. His head practically hit the roof and his seat was, from what she could tell, pushed all the way back. Yeah, he was a big man, strong and fit, but it was his hands that gave her pause. They were large, the nails clipped and blunt. Small white scars crisscrossed his knuckles, blaring white against the back of each dark hand. Those hands could cause pain, those hands could kill, but those hands could also protect and give pleasure. A warm feeling tingled through her body as she considered just what his hands were capable of. As her eyes drifted back to his face, she was shocked to find him staring at her, the light from the dashboard making his eyes glow. Okaaay....this is awkward.

"You gonna answer that?"

"Huh..." Frowning into his eyes, she jumped when her cell phone rang by her feet. Feeling like the biggest idiot, going all gooey eyed over a hot guy, she grabbed her bag rummaging through it. Flipping the phone open, she peeked over relieved that Damon's eyes were focused back on the road. "Hello."

Damon stopped at a red light trying to get it together. He had felt her gaze on him and turned to see if she was okay and what he saw in her eyes was enough to flame his blood to the point he almost pulled the car over. He knew the first time he saw her running into the warehouse that she was different and every protective instinct he possessed jumped out and bit him on the ass. The sight of her black eye that first night sent a killing rage through him. He had almost killed that dumbass human, Chad, for just being disrespectful. He had seen enough mated males of his species to know the signs, but he had no ambition to be mated and sure as hell not to a human.

"That was Mitch." Nicole broke through his thoughts as did the asswipe behind them blowing their horn since the light had turned green. "I need to go to the Children's Hospital. There's a sixteen year old who has been placed into our care."

"You need to rest Nicole." Damon zoomed through the light. "Call Mitch back and tell him you can't make it. He can get someone else."

"Ah...no."

"Did you tell Mitch what happened tonight?" Damon persisted.

"Nope." Nicole flipped her phone open again undoing her seatbelt. "Yeah I need a cab at the corner of..." Nicole practically had her face pressed to the windshield trying to see a street sign.

"Hang up the phone." When Nicole ignored him while reading the street sign to the cab dispatcher, he reached over and grabbed the phone.

"Hey," she tried to grab it back.

"Disregard that. She will not need your services." He snapped the phone closed and tossed it into her lap. "Put your seatbelt back on."

"If you don't stop this car, I'm going to get out the first chance I get," she warned, her hand easing to the handle. "I'm fine, Damon. You need to let me do my job."

35

"I said, put your seatbelt on." He stopped at another light. Before she could escape, he reached over, slammed her door shut, and firmly snapped her seatbelt back in place. Without moving back, his breath fanned across her face moving wisps of hair. "I'll take you."

"Thank you." Her breath mingled with his, their eyes held for a second. When he moved back to his seat and pulled a U-turn, she relaxed. Ah yeah, this was getting really awkward. How was she supposed to work with the guy when all she wanted to do was leap across and straddle him? Good Lord, she had to get a grip. Her job was too important to her to mess up with a bunch of hot meaningless sex... and knowing what sat across from her, she knew it would be hotter than hell.

Chapter 4

Damon pulled into an empty spot in the emergency room parking lot at Children's Hospital. Grabbing her bag, Nicole headed toward the door noticing all the police cruisers. Glancing at Damon, she saw his expression was as confused and concerned as hers. The doors slid open and they were hit with a blast of cold air as they entered the emergency room. It was packed with anxious parents with crying kids, all waiting to be seen. Seeing Mitch, she headed his way.

"Excuse me," a blonde woman behind the sign-in desk spoke loudly trying to stop her and Damon.

"I'm with them," Nicole kept walking and pointed over her shoulder, "and he's with me."

The woman threw up her hands. "I need to see some ID," she shouted after them.

Ignoring the woman, Nicole walked up to Mitch, nodding at a few of the police officers she knew. "What's going on Mitch?"

"We have a hell of a mess is what's going on." Mitch ran his hand down his face, the shadows under his puffy eyes making him look older and more tired than she'd ever seen him. "We have a 16 year old vampire in there who killed both of his foster parents, human parents."

"Oh God." Nicole tried to peek around him to see if she could see the kid.

"It took ten officers to bring him down and he got a little roughed up so they brought him here. Now he has a nurse and is threatening to kill her if they don't let him go. They're going to take him out." Mitch stepped back getting out of way of the hospital staff pulling Nicole with him.

"Who is it Mitch?" God, if it was one of her cases she was going to freak out right here and now.

"It's Stevie Richardson," Mitch glared at the floor. "It's Chad's case and I can't get a hold of him, so I called you. I want you to try to talk him down Nicole."

"No!" Damon had kept quiet up to this point. No way was he going to let Nicole get anywhere near this kid. He knew how unstable a cornered vampire could be and he had no doubt that this kid would kill. Hell, he already had. "I'll take care of this."

Nicole grabbed his arm. "How Damon? By going in there and turning all bad warrior vamp on the kid? Stevie was one of my cases until Chad threw a fit because he wanted to work with him and place him. I gave up the case. Now I wish I wouldn't have. Stevie's a good kid. Something isn't right about this whole situation and if you go in there, we may never find out what it is."

"Do you have a death wish?" Damon glared at her, jaw clinched. "You *are* human. What don't you understand about that Nicole? You have no power over our kind."

"You're right," Nicole nodded. "Not with violence I don't, but I can get through to these kids, and I'm not going to let him get hurt. Something triggered this and we need to find out what it is before it's too late."

Damon understood, he really did, but he didn't want Nicole going anywhere near this kid who had already killed. Stevie had already had a taste of blood lust, and he'd be damned if he tasted any of Nicole's.

Nicole stopped listening as her mind began to work. She could do this without violence. She knew she could. She had done it before. Seeing a teenager walking down the hall toward them drinking a Dew, she headed toward him. "Hey," she approached with a smile and cash she'd dug out of her pocket in her hand. "I'll buy that t-shirt off you for twenty-five bucks."

"Seriously?" the kid eyed the money that she flashed in her hand.

"About as serious as that Dew rotting out every tooth in your head." Glancing down at her feet, then his, she took more money out. "I'll give you sixty for the shirt and shoes."

"Hell, yeah!" He started stripping out of his shirt and shoes, stumbling around in his haste to get the money in his hand.

"Thanks." Nicole pushed the money into his hand, and grabbed her purchase. Toeing off her boots, she starting stripping out of her long sleeved dress shirt she'd worn to the club.

"Hey, what the hell are you doing?" Damon rushed over, grabbing the shirt, pulling it back down; not that he would mind seeing what she was hiding under her clothes. A quick glance around said that there were others with that same thought. Yeah, not fuckin' likely.

"I've got a sports bra underneath this. Now let go." She shrugged from his hold and continued changing.

Damon growled baring his fangs at the kid and police officers who stood watching her undress. "Dammit Nicole." He pushed her behind him to give her some privacy. "Couldn't you have done that in the bathroom?"

After putting on the rumpled AC/DC t-shirt that smelled awful, she grabbed the shoes and put them on without untying them. "No time, and it's not like I'm going to ignite a lust fest in my sports bra. Geez vamp, chill."

Damon glared down at the top of her head as she rummaged in her bag. "What the hell is changing your shirt and shoes going to do to help with this situation?"

Gathering her hair into a ponytail, she wrapped the rubber band around it then stood. "I don't want to look like a social worker. I want him comfortable around me. I want to be on his level."

Damon snorted shaking his head. "Human, you are crazy."

"As a loon," she smiled as she shoved her bag hard into his stomach and walked toward Mitch. "Okay, ready."

"Nice outfit," Mitch shook his head. This is why he didn't fire Nicole, as bad as he wanted to at times. She went the extra mile to do her job and that was something rare indeed. "Just don't get killed. Okay. The paperwork will be a bitch."

"Love you too Mitch," Nicole snorted when Damon grumbled loudly. What was his problem?

Walking through the doors, Nicole gasped. At least ten uniformed cops surrounded a curtained partition with their guns drawn. Her eyes then focused on their target. A typical teenager with blonde spiky hair, his eyes huge in his pale face. Not so typical was his scrawny arm wrapped around an older nurse's throat. Slowly, she made her way in front, but out of the line of fire. Obviously, Mitch had informed them that she was going to try to talk the boy down because no one tried to stop her.

"Don't come any closer," his fangs gleamed under the florescent lights, his arm tightening around the nurse's throat, making her cry out.

Nicole put her hand out, "I won't Stevie."

"My name is Steve!" he spat out. "My fucking name is Steve."

"Okay, Steve." Nicole dropped her arm. "Listen to me Steve. We have ourselves in a bad situation here and it doesn't look too good from where I'm standing and I'm sure it's not any better from where you are either."

"Yeah, ya think?" He shuffled back a step dragging the nurse with him.

"If you let her go," Nicole motioned to the nurse, "everyone will leave. Then me and you can talk about what happened."

"Bullshit." This time there was less anger in his voice, more hope in his eyes.

Nicole heard the cursing behind her, but ignored it. If she could get him to let the nurse go, then these guys were going to have to give something up. Getting rid of all these cops, was going to be the key to ending this standoff. "One thing you need to know about me Steve is that I don't bullshit." Nicole stood firm, staring at the boy, willing him to believe that she was trying to save his life. "I want answers to what happened tonight so I can help you. I think I know what might have happened, but we need to talk. We can't do that with you holding that nurse."

"Why would you want to help me?" His eyes nervously flicking around to the guns. "You're human, right? So what do you care about me for? Huh?"

"It's my job to help you, plus I understand more than you know." Nicole felt nervous beads of sweat popping out on her forehead. God, this could turn ugly so fast.

"Are you kidding me?" he screamed, jerking the woman closer to him. "Are you like that other social worker?"

"Who was your social worker?" Nicole knew exactly who it was, but didn't want him to know she knew. When he didn't answer, she sighed, "Is his name Chad?"

"Yeah and he never would call me back. Told me to hang in there and that I wasn't trying hard enough to fit in. I needed to try harder and now look where I am."

Bitter bile rose up her throat threatening to choke her. Knowing Chad had indeed arrived, because she heard his pansy ass voice, she turned to glare at him. "Look Steve," Nicole said loudly turning her attention back to the boy, "I'm sorry you got stuck with him."

"You're a social worker?" he snorted and rolled his eyes to the ceiling dropping his head back. "God, just kill me now."

41

"Everyone get out." She turned to Mitch, "Get everyone out."

"Nicole," Mitch warned, shaking his head.

Turning back to Steve, she took a step forward. "If I get everyone out of here, will you let her go and talk to me?"

Steve leveled his gaze back to her. "Why should I trust you?"

"Because I just became your new hostage." Nicole heard Damon cursing behind her, but ignored it. "I really want to hear your story. I'm not saying you're not in trouble for what you did, but at least everyone will know the real reason behind it and we can work on getting you a good defense team together. My boss has a lot of connections."

"You like AC/DC?" he asked eyeing her shirt.

"Seen them every year they came to Cincinnati," Nicole grinned, then shot an I told you so look at Damon.

"Yeah, they kick ass," he nodded seeming more at ease. "I'll let her go if you get them out."

"Done." Nicole turned to Mitch. "Keep someone ready around the corner if this goes bad," she whispered so only those close to her could hear.

"What the hell are you doing Nicole?" Mitch demanded as the chief of police came barreling toward them.

"Can someone tell me who put this woman in charge?" The chief was looking at her as if she was a piece of crap on the bottom of his finely polished shoe.

"No one did, Sir." Nicole turned back to see how Steve was taking all of this commotion. His eyes stayed steady on her, still holding his arm around the poor nurse's throat. "I can talk him down, but not with guns pointing at him from all directions. I can also get the nurse released, but I have to gain his trust and the trust I have gained so far, which isn't much, is trickling away the more we stand here trying to figure out who's in charge."

The chief eyed the situation with a stern frown. "If this goes bad, it's on your head."

Nicole nodded, figuring as much and knew, because of that fact, she wasn't backing down. She never did before so why start now? She watched as the chief gave the orders and the officers started backing away slowly. Mitch and the others followed suit, until everyone was evacuated but Damon. "You need to leave Damon."

"I can take care of this Nicole," Damon stared over her head at the young vampire and knew he could take him out in a blink of an eye. The nurse may suffer for it, but it was a chance he was willing to take. He did not want Nicole in danger. His whole body burned at the thought of her getting hurt.

"I'm sure you can, but I still need to talk to him and I know I can get more out of him than those guys down at the police station. They still fear your kind and would rather lock him away than find out what really happened. You know this Damon. I could find out a lot from him." She hoped he would see her reasoning.

"I'm not leaving." Damon turned her and pushed her toward Steve. "If he doesn't go for that, then the deal is off and I'll take him out."

Nicole nodded knowing Damon wasn't going to back down on this either. At least Steve seemed to be easing up a little with the cops and guns gone. "Okay Steve. I did my part, now you need to do yours and let her go."

"What about him?" Steve nodded his head at Damon.

"Well you see that's a problem. My friend is very protective and wants to make sure we just talk. " Nicole turned and shot a glare at Damon who cocked an eyebrow. "He promised he wouldn't interfere as long as things remained calm, which I don't see that being a problem. So do we have a deal?"

"He's a vampire?" Steve unwrapped his arm from the nurse's neck, but kept a hand on her shoulder.

"Yes he is," Nicole nodded. "Is that a problem?"

"Just tell him to stay out of my head. I feel him in there probing around," he watched Damon suspiciously.

"Done." Nicole looked over at Damon, "Please?"

Damon inclined his head to her then turned his focus on the boy. "Steve I'll do as you ask, but if you make one move to hurt her, it *will* be the last move you ever make. She's trying to help you and is putting her life and job on the line. If you decide to take yourself down, she will not go down with you."

Steve swallowed hard and nodded, letting the nurse go. She ran to Nicole, who quietly told her to leave through the door behind Damon. Nicole turned and walked slowly toward Steve. "Okay, now we can figure out what happened and what we're going to do about it."

Steve took one last look at Damon as he sat on the bed putting his head in both of his hands with a huge sigh. "God, I don't know where to start."

Nicole walked up and sat on the end of the hospital bed. She didn't have to turn to know that Damon came closer. "Listen Steve," she sighed. "I'm going to be straight up with you. I know your file. I was supposed to be your case manager, but Chad wanted it so it was given to him. I'm sorry things didn't turn out for you under Chad's care."

Steve snorted lifting his head up to meet her stare. "No it didn't turn out, obviously."

Nicole nodded. The poor kid. He already had so many strikes against

44

him before he was turned. He would be sixteen for the rest of his vampire life. No way would she want to be sixteen forever. He was the only child of parents who couldn't handle the matrimony of marriage and called it quits when he was five. Raised by his mother, who was a heavy drug user and known well by the police, he had spent time in the system on and off for most of his adolescent life. At sixteen, his mom kicked him out and he landed on the streets where he got caught up with the wrong people and was turned. Getting caught by the police for stealing a car, he was charged, but being a minor, he was to be released into his mother's custody. Problem was, his mother never showed up to take him. He was now a ward of the state and what a bang up job they had done for the kid.

"Why did you kill your adoptive parents Steve?" Nicole cocked her head to the side ready to listen. "Let's start there."

Taking one last look at Damon, he rubbed his hands together back and forth. "I didn't do it." He looked back to Nicole to see what kind of reaction she had to that little tidbit. When her features showed nothing, he continued. "There was someone else there, but I didn't see who it was."

"Okay," Nicole sat up straighter. "Did you hear anything that would give you a clue to who it was?"

He shook his head. "I came in through the kitchen after work. I have a part time job after school. They didn't have much for me to do at Wilson's Garage so I headed home early. I was in the kitchen getting ready to grab a drink from the fridge when I heard my mom talking loudly from the other room. She was always quiet, so it surprised me to hear her voice raised. So I walked into the hall and stood there figuring she and my dad was fighting and hoped it wasn't about me."

Nicole nodded her head in understanding. Poor kid. Wanting to belong, but afraid he never would. Finding a family, but afraid it would disappear any minute. "Go on Steve."

His eyes focused over her head. She didn't know if he stared at Damon or nothing. "They were in the office with the door shut. I heard her saying that they changed their minds. They didn't need the money anymore and that they were not going to agree to anything. I heard another voice yelling at her telling her to shut up."

"Male or female?" Damon asked, moving closer. Nicole flinched, hoping Damon's question wouldn't stop Steve from continuing. When Steve looked at Damon, she knew that wasn't going to be the case. The kid wanted this off his chest.

"Male, and it wasn't my dad." Steve leaned his head back and sighed again. "My dad told this person that under no circumstance would he be selling my blood to anyone."

Nicole gave him a minute of quiet and was surprised to find Damon standing beside her, his arms crossed staring at the boy. "What happened next, son?"

Steve frowned at Damon, but didn't comment on him calling him son. "I heard the other person saying they were making a huge mistake and then I heard my mom scream and all kinds of noises came from the office. I ran, but couldn't get the door open fast enough."

Nicole laid her hand on the boy's foot. "I'm so sorry, Steve." Nicole wanted to scream at the injustice of it all.

"God, it was awful. Neither one of them were moving. My dad was lying over my mom like he was trying to protect her. My dad wasn't breathing and I tried pulling him off her to see if she was still alive. I slipped in the blood and fell. I got him off her, but she was dead." Tears of blood ran down his face. "Even though we had issues, I would never hurt them. They were trying, but I'm just not used to rules and they had so many. I heard them talking last night. My mom was saying they had made a mistake and I thought they were talking about me, but now I don't think they were. God, why did this happen?"

Nicole crawled across the bed and took him into her arms, holding him tight. "I don't know Steve, but we will find who did this."

He pulled away staring at her in surprise, "You....believe me?"

"Yeah, I do," Nicole nodded. "And I'm going to have you stay here while I go talk to the police. Okay? We will get this worked out, but you are going to have to tell them everything that you told us and hopefully something else will come to you before then."

"Why are you doing this?" Steve wondered aloud, and then smirked. "Oh, yeah, I forgot....it's your job, just like that Chad asshole."

Nicole had moved off the bed and grabbed her bag. "It is my job, but I'm better at my job than Chad, so please don't compare me to him, cause I really like you." She smiled when he laughed.

"Yeah...okay." He took the card she handed him.

"Don't hesitate to call me, okay?" Nicole turned serious. "I answer my calls and return them always, no matter how big or small the issue. You said you kept calling Chad, but he wouldn't return your calls? Can I ask why you were trying to call him?"

Steve sighed, "At first, things were real hard. I mean, we just didn't hit it off. They weren't bad or anything, but I just didn't think it was going to work. Then one day me and them went to the zoo and had a blast. After that, things started to change for the better. When Chad did his visits, he never talked to me, just my parents, and then after the last one, I found my mom crying after he left. She wouldn't tell me what happened, but said not to worry about it, things were fine." Steve shrugged his shoulders. "I don't know. I just didn't like him much."

Nicole smiled, "Can't blame ya there."

"I can't go back into the system again," Steve wiped his cheeks with the back of his hand. "I am going to outlive every parent if they're human, and I can't do this again."

"Let's work one thing out at a time," Nicole replied. "Okay? Now stay here and let me go get things straightened out."

Steve nodded, then grinned, "Do you really like AC/DC?"

She hiked her bag up on her shoulder. "Sure do," she winked. "I'll take you to see them next time they're in town."

"Seriously?" The first real smile flashed across the kids face. "Cool."

"Seriously." Nicole walked past Damon and touched his arm. "I'll be right back."

Nicole walked out into the hall and saw only the police and Mitch. Everyone else had been evacuated.

"What happened?" The chief walked to her, "Where is he?"

"Damon is with him." Nicole turned to Mitch. "He said that he didn't kill them, that someone else was in the house and I believe him." She continued to explain everything that Steve had told her and Damon.

"We still have to bring him in, Mitch. He did hold a nurse hostage and if she wants to press charges there is nothing I can do about that." The chief stated, but raised his hand before Nicole could blast him. "But he will be well taken care of."

"Damn straight he will," Nicole replied hotly. "I want him transferred under me, Mitch."

"Now wait a damn minute," Chad piped in pushing his way toward them. "I am not going to release this case over."

"He is not a case," Nicole growled, sounding like Damon. "He is a boy who could not get hold of you when he needed to."

"Now you listen here you little..." Chad got in her face grabbing her shirt in his fist before Mitch could stop him.

"Didn't I warn you about this?" Damon stepped between her and Chad knocking his hand away from Nicole. "Steve is no longer anyone's.

48

He is a part of the VC Warriors."

"What?" Nicole sucked in a strangling breath choking herself. Seeing Steve's beaming smile, she saw that he was happy at the new development. "Serious?"

He turned to the chief, "One of my partners is going to be coming by the station. You may ask Steve any questions you have to ask and follow your process, but as soon as you're finished, we'll take him back to our headquarters."

The chief nodded his head then looked at Mitch. "Can he do that?"

"Looks like he just did." Mitch patted Damon on the back, "This is a good thing you're doing my friend."

Damon looked uncomfortable at Mitch's praise. Turning to the boy, he placed his hand on his shoulder, "You're under our protection now, son. You go with the chief and answer anything they ask. You have nothing to hide. Duncan will be there soon. You'll know him. He's a big, ugly son of a bitch. You can tell him I said that," Damon grinned down at the boy.

"This is total bullshit," Chad ranted. "How can you let this happen, Mitch?" I'm really getting sick and tired of that bitch interfering in my cases," he pointed in Nicole's face.

"I have given you fair warning human." Damon advanced toward Chad his fist clinched. "If you ever touch her again, you *will* regret it."

Mitch somehow stopped Damon from reaching Chad. "You're on report, Chad." Mitch felt his feet sliding as the huge vampire continued his advancement toward Chad. "You better get the hell out of here before I let him loose on you. I want you in my office first thing in the morning."

"You can kiss my ass, Mitch. I quit. I don't need your shit anymore." Chad leaned toward Nicole. "You better watch that sweet ass of yours

Callahan. You have no clue what you've done."

They all watched Chad stomp out the door throwing his ID badge on the floor.

"You know, I can't say I'm sorry to see him go." Mitch turned his attention back to Damon, "You okay my man?"

"No," Damon answered, his eyes wicked black. "I want to kill the son of a bitch."

"He isn't worth it." Nicole looked at her watch. This had been the longest night of her life. It seemed like weeks had passed since she had gotten tackled on the dance floor at Sub Zero.

As if reading her mind, Damon turned back toward Mitch. "Can you take care of the kid until Duncan gets there? Nicole had a rough night before this even started and I would like to get her home."

"What the hell happened before this?" Mitch looked Nicole over with a frown.

"Nothing really, just got tackled by Damon and some other dude on the dance floor at Sub Zero," Nicole waved her hand around as if it wasn't a big deal.

"Yeah...riiight," Mitch replied rolling his eyes. "Yeah, I got him. Take her home."

Nicole waved to Steve who was listening to one of the officers, but his eyes were fixed on the door Chad had walked out of. Seeing Nicole waving, his smile filled with gratitude as he waved back.

Yawning for the hundredth time since leaving the hospital, Nicole covered her mouth. "Man, I am getting too old for this staying up late stuff." Walking up to her apartment, she fit her key into the door, hoping that her nosy neighbor was snug in her bed, fast asleep. With a sigh of relief, she walked in to see Pam sleeping on the couch, lightly snoring. She had sent a text to Pam on the way to the hospital to tell her what was going on, but Pam had still wanted to come and said she'd wait. Dropping her bag by the door, she turned to Damon.

"Make sure you lock up when I leave." His golden gaze searched hers. "You were great tonight. I have never seen a human so determined to save one of ours."

Nicole nodded, looking away embarrassed. She didn't feel like she had done anything special. She did what was right. "Thanks." She walked up to him, "You did pretty good yourself. What you're doing for Steve is wonderful and so much more than I could have ever done for him."

"Goodnight Nicole."

Before he could leave, she walked up to him; reaching up on her tiptoes, she grabbed the front of his shirt pulling him closer to her and kissed him lightly on the cheek. "For a badass dude, you really are a sweet guy."

His eyes dropped to her lips and he lowered his head slowly. "And for a badass chick, you're pretty sweet yourself. I won't tell if you don't."

She chuckled softly, her eyes glued to his lips, "Deal."

"Deal," he whispered back, and then dropped his head lower and caught her lips with his; his tongue licked its way inside, meeting hers. With one hand on her lower back, he pulled her up his body and deepened the kiss. Before her hands could make it up his broad shoulders to his hair, he set her down and walked out the door closing it firmly behind him. "Lock it," he demanded behind the closed door, his voice sounding much deeper.

Nicole jumped and did as he said, staring at the door, her hands at her lips. "Whoa," she whispered, touching her still tingling lips.

"Whoa is right," Pam chuckled from the couch making Nicole jump and squeal. "That was damn hot. Girlfriend, I thought he was going to take you right there."

Nicole's face turned ten shades of red. "Shut up, Pam." Walking to the bathroom, she slammed the door on Pam's loud laughter, a huge grin spreading across her flushed face.

Chapter 5

Damon slammed his way into headquarters, pissed at himself. What the hell was he doing kissing Nicole like that? This was not good. Well, the kiss had been more than good. It had been soul shattering good. Hell, he had to sit in the parking lot of headquarters to get himself under control before walking in with his cock waving hidey-ho to everyone. That would have gone over real swell with the guys. God, her scent and sweet taste was enough to...he broke that thought off. No need to go down that road again or he'd be back in his car waiting out another hard-on. Nothing could come of it and he knew it. She was human and he wasn't, that was the bottom line. Thoughts of changing her scattered through his mind, but he closed that off. No way was that happening and she wasn't a woman who would be happy with a wham bam thank you ma'am moment.

"What the hell's wrong with you?" Jared stomped down the steps from the upstairs living area. All the warriors had places of their own, but headquarters also housed each of them for late nights and emergency situations.

"Nothing!" Damon snapped. "Where's the kid?"

Jared tossed a nod up the steps. "Checking out his new room." Jared headed toward the kitchen area. "Good kid."

"Yeah." Damon grabbed a beer out of the fridge. They drank and ate just like anyone else, but the need for blood set them apart, among a few other things, like living forever. Warriors could actually go weeks before needing to feed and they had females who were hired for that purpose. "So what did you find out from Jamison?"

Jared placed a whole baked chicken in front of him, along with his beer. "Nothing yet. Phillip is working on him now."

Damon shook his head when Jared offered him some chicken. Damn, the vamp could eat. "Think I'll go down and help." He needed something to take his mind off the beautiful human who was turning his world inside out.

"Need to get blondie out of your system?" Jared chuckled when Damon flipped him off as he walked out the door.

"Stay out of my head, Jared."

"Don't have to read your mind bro." Jared called out after him. "It's written all over your face."

Stepping into the room with a two-way mirror, he stopped next to Duncan. "Any luck finding out who the slime was after?" Damon watched Phillip walk up behind Jamison who was tied to a chair with silver chains.

"Not yet," Duncan sighed. "He's a tough one to crack. Those damn silver chains have got to be killing the son of a bitch."

Damon nodded, staring at Jamison's wrist. Silver wouldn't kill them unless it was shot into their bodies, but it burned like a bitch and kept them immobile. "Care if I take a turn?"

"Hell, you might as well. So far none of us have had any luck." Duncan buzzed the door.

"Well...well. Look who we have here, boys and girls." Jamison shot Phillip a smug look when he said girls. "The one and only Damon DeMasters, the warrior of all warriors."

Phillip growled, but turned and walked out leaving Damon and Jamison alone.

Damon's smile was cold, "Jealous much?"

Jamison snorted. "So what do you want to know, warrior?" Jamison's eyes gleamed under the fluorescent lights. "What I've been doing since we last met, maybe, or how about, oh I don't know, how I plan on fucking that cute little human you were so worried about at the club?"

Damon felt his body tense as anger tried to override his common sense. His cold smile stayed in place. He would not, could not, give Jamison any hint of weakness on his part. It could be deadly for Nicole. "What makes you think I want to know about your disgusting love life Jamison?"

"Oh, okay we gonna play that way, huh?" Jamison grinned, amusement playing in his eyes. "Okay, I'll play."

Damon walked around the table and leaned against it, arms crossed. "Who was your target?"

"Well, you see, I just told you." Jamison watched him closely, his keen killer eyes not missing a beat.

"What do you want with the woman?" Damon was fucking proud of himself, his voice didn't even deepen with the rage he felt.

Jamison chuckled, "Damn warrior, you're good. Some might think you didn't care for the little human." He laughed more, sounding like a deranged lunatic. "But we both know differently, don't we, DeMasters? God, this is just too much."

"Cut the shit and answer the question." Damon turned cold eyes on him.

"I told you that too." Jamison rolled his eyes. "I want to fuck her and then do what I do best, kill the little bitch and collect my money. Seems she's a little too good at her job and people are taking notice."

"Who hired you?" Damon thought he deserved an Academy Award for his performance. He wanted nothing more than to lean back and beat the living hell out of the bastard.

"Ah, now that I can't tell you. You know, assassin and client confidentiality, and all that shit. Gotta follow the rules or I don't get paid. Have you ever had a human, warrior?"

Damon ignored him. "You know you won't be getting shit since you'll be locked up here, so you might as well come clean."

Jamison followed suit and ignored Damon, something he would probably later regret. "Have you ever had a human, warrior? Ahhh... let me tell you, they're sweet. Their scent and softness is something that draws you in," he sniffed the air as he spoke. "And I can tell you, nothing smells as sweet as your Nicole."

Damon lost all control at the sound of her name on the bastard's lips. Jamming his hand around Jamison's throat, he snarled. "Who put the hit out?"

Jamison struggled against the hold, but Damon's hand and the chains kept him in place. "Fuck you, warrior," he wheezed. "Go ahead and kill me. It won't stop until she's dead. Someone will replace me. Better me screwing her than someone else. I'd at least make sure she enjoyed it before I killed her."

Damon didn't hesitate. He snapped the bastards head off with his bare hands. "Wrong answer."

Duncan, Phillip and Jared burst into the room. "Holy shit, Damon," Jared skid to a stop as Jamison's bald head bounced past his well-worn boots.

"What the hell did you do that for?" Duncan demanded.

"It's the best way to kill a vampire," Damon answered with a dead calm he didn't feel. "And he had to die."

All three turned and watched Damon stroll out the door not looking back. "Remind me of this the next time I piss him off." Jared glanced back at the headless vamp. "Have you ever seen anyone snap someone's head off like that?"

"No." Both Duncan and Phillip answered in unison, eyeing the head under Jared's foot.

One of Jamison's hands twitched. "Okay, now *that* is creepy." Jared shivered then kicked Jamison's head under the chair his body still occupied. "And I have seen some creepy shit."

Chapter 6

Nicole was nervous as she headed inside the warehouse. She hoped her sleepless night didn't show on her face. This would be the first time she had seen Damon since their kiss, and she really didn't know what to think. Confidence, where men were concerned, was not a strong point for her. Buddies she could do, but once it crossed the buddy line she was doomed.

Yep, this was not going to be fun.

Her stomach fluttered so badly, she thought she was going to throw up. Wow, she was such a wuss. She needed to grow a pair and stop freaking out. It was just a kiss...get a grip. Slapping her hand against the door, she pushed her way in.

"Hey," Pam smiled, seeing Nicole walk in the door.

"Why didn't you wake me before you left this morning?" Nicole set her bag down and followed Pam out onto the mat. "I would have made us some of my famous chocolate chip pancakes."

"You were sleeping so good I didn't want to wake you." She rubbed her flat stomach, "And I'm getting a little pudgy."

"Ha! There isn't an ounce of fat on you," Nicole snorted. "Witch."

Pam laughed, and then nudged her. "I haven't seen Romeo, so stop straining them eyeballs."

"What? I was just seeing if Mitch was here yet," she lied. They sat on the mat, facing each other, stretching and talking. "Did you buy your dress yet for the charity dance?"

"No. I figured we could go together sometime this week?" Pam was lounging more than stretching.

"Bet my dress from last year still fits." Nicole bent one knee and stretched over the other leg.

"Ohhh no you don't!" Pam shook her head. "Over my dead body will you wear a repeat dress, especially accepting an award."

"Ugh, I forgot about that." Wrinkling her nose she frowned. "I don't need an award. This is my job. If I didn't have to pay bills, I would do it for free."

"Yeah, well speak for yourself, Mother Teresa," Pam chuckled. Nicole laughed. Getting up, she turned and the laughter stuck in her throat. Walking out of the back room, was Damon with the most beautiful woman she had ever seen fixing his shirt collar. It was like staring at a car wreck; she couldn't look away. His eyes lifted from the woman and looked straight at her. Nicole knew then and there, she was in deep trouble. The fluttering in her stomach fell quiet, replaced with a hard knot.

"I'm so sorry, Nicole," Pam whispered.

Nicole looked away from Damon with a shrug, turning to Pam with a smile, trying to keep it together. "It was just a kiss. No big deal." She didn't know who she was trying to convince, herself or Pam.

"Come on. Let's go beat the crap out of Jared," Pam grabbed her arm, throwing a dark look over her shoulder at Damon, who was still staring at Nicole.

The workout was pretty laid back. They worked mostly on cardio and a few easy self-defense techniques. Damon stayed away from Nicole and helped everyone but her and Pam. Nicole had watched the woman leave and knew she fell short. Way short. The woman was a ten and a half, while Nicole put herself around a five on the hotness scale, if that. The sad part was if she had to pick a woman Damon would be with, it was that woman, not someone like her. Wow, what a total self-confidence killer. Seeing Damon walking off the mat where Mitch was waving her over, she sighed and headed that way.

"We need to talk to you," Mitch frowned, not looking happy at all, which wasn't much of a stretch.

For a second, Nicole blanched as she remembered the kiss. She quickly pushed the panic and thought aside as she realized Damon wouldn't have blabbed about that. Obviously, it was not as memorable to him as it was her. God, get over it already...it was just a freakin kiss. So what if it just about set her panties on fire.

"Nicole?" Mitch snapped his fingers in front of her face.

"Huh?" Nicole jerked her head toward Mitch, not wanting to even glance at Damon. "What?"

"Didn't you hear what I just said?" Mitch sighed, giving her the 'getting ready to bitch you out' eyeball.

"Mitch, just spit it out." Nicole felt her face flame. Damn, she had to get her head on straight.

"Well I did, but you had your head up your ass."

"I'm tired Mitch. I've had maybe four hours of sleep and I'm hungry. You of all people know what I'm like with a lack of sleep and no food." Nicole rubbed her eyebrow with the back of her hand. She just wanted to get out of there, grab a heart attack in a sack from the closest fast food joint and then crawl into bed and sleep until her alarm clock went off on Monday morning, signaling the start of another long week. "And before you ask, no, I don't want you to throw me a pity party. So let's just get this over with before I go PMS on you."

Mitch cursed. He was used to her long speeches, but by the look on Damon, Jared and Duncan's face, they were shocked if not a little amused. Jared was the first to burst out laughing. "Damn Mitch, we do not want to go there."

"Believe me, I know," Mitch smirked. "Been there, done that, more than you even know."

Nicole threw up her hands walking away. "I'm going home. Text me."

"Get your ass back here, Callahan," Mitch sighed, looking as tired as she felt. "We have a problem."

"Is Steve okay?" Nicole woke up fast.

Damon shook his head in amazement. Thinking of others first was one of things that had drawn him to her.

"The man we took down at the club last night was after someone." Jared began, glancing at Damon then back to Nicole.

"Yeah, I know. Damon told me." Nicole wasn't putting two and two together. "So, did he get away from you?"

Jared choked a chuckle back. "Ah...no." His head did though, but he kept that to himself. "We know who his target was."

Still Nicole stared at them, even Damon. "And..."

"It was you," Mitch added when Jared didn't.

"Me?" That took her mind off Damon real quick. "Why would he be after me? I've never seen that man before in my life."

"It seems someone thinks you are doing your job too well." Jared again eyed Damon, who was still staring at Nicole.

"As of today, you're on a leave of absence." Mitch put on his boss hat.

"No," Nicole shook her head. "First of all, this has to be a mistake. You got it wrong." She looked at the three vampires then back to Mitch. "I am not going on a leave of absence, Mitch."

"Yes, you are, and I am not budging on this, Nicole." Okay, he was serious. He just used her first name. He never, ever did that.

"Is there any family you could go stay with?" Duncan asked before Nicole could tear into Mitch.

Shaking her head, Nicole replied, "No, there isn't."

"I'll call my brother and see if you can stay with him and his wife in Michigan." Mitch started dialing.

Nicole stood there speechless. Suddenly, her life was spiraling out of control, or at least out of her control, and if Damon didn't stop staring at her, she was going to scream. Grabbing Mitch's phone, she snapped it shut and tossed it back to him. "While I appreciate you doing that Mitch, it's a waste of time. I'm a big girl who can make big girl decisions, and have been for most of my life." She turned to Duncan, "I really don't see a problem if you got the guy. Right?"

There was some nervous shuffling of feet and looking away. "We had him," Duncan looked at Damon.

"So that's the problem? He got away?" Nicole did not like where this was heading and seeing three nervous vampire warriors was not helping matters.

"No, I killed him," Damon replied with ease. "And someone will take his place."

Nicole stepped back, stunned. He killed him.

"We need to get you somewhere safe until we can find out who put the hit on you." Duncan looked at Mitch, "Call your brother."

"No, Mitch." Nicole tore her gaze from Damon. "I'm not going into hiding. I don't understand any of this, but I know I'm not going to run and leave my job. I'm not stupid. I'll be careful and lock my doors, but right now, I need to get home and feed Ren and Stimpy." Why the hell she said that she didn't know. All she knew was she had to get away from them and the only thing that came to mind was feeding her turtles. Grabbing her bag, she raced out the door to her car.

"Who the fuck is Ren and Stimpy?" Jared turned to look at everyone, confused.

Damon ignored him as he pushed out the door behind Nicole.

"Let it go Mitch." Hearing heavy footsteps coming up behind her, Nicole didn't even turn around figuring it was Mitch. "I'm not leaving and I *will* be at work Monday morning." Opening the door, she threw her bag in the backseat, got in and slammed the door.

Damon put both hands on the hood of her car, leaning down so his face was in line with her window. "We need to talk." He opened her door.

"No, I don't think we do." Nicole went to close her door, but he stopped it with his hand.

"You need to listen to Mitch and get out of town for a while." Damon leaned down closer to her level.

Feeling more tired than she ever had in her life, she turned to look at him, laying her head on the steering wheel. "I can't afford to take off work Damon. Who will pay my bills? Who will feed my turtles?" She just stared at him, as if she could find the answers in his eyes. "I don't have anyone and I'm not going to live with strangers." That was all her life had consisted of growing up. No, she wouldn't put herself in that position again.

Damon rubbed his eyes and sighed, "This is your life we're talking about."

"You're right. It is my life and this isn't your problem, Damon." Nicole started her car with a rattle and puff of smoke. "Now, please shut my door, so I can go home and go to bed." She wanted to add, so he could go back to his girlfriend, but didn't. She wasn't in high school anymore. She really didn't know what she felt for this man and she was afraid to find out. A broken heart was definitely something she didn't need right now.

"Dammit Nicole, get out of the car before I pull you out." Damon stepped back and that was the break she needed. Slamming into gear, she lifted her foot off the brake and took off, her door slamming shut from the force of the car speeding off.

"Pull me out, my ass." Nicole snorted then glanced in her rear view mirror expecting to see him standing in her dust, but to her horror he was running right up behind her leaping into the air before landing on the top of her car with a loud boom. Screaming, she let go of the steering wheel, her hands flying to her face. Covering her eyes, she slammed the brakes. "Are you freakin crazy?!" she screamed, afraid to look in case she saw him splattered all over the hood of her car.

Jumping down, Damon threw open her door almost yanking it off the hinges. "Get out."

Turning her head, she peeked through her fingers, hoping to find him in one piece and not a bloody mess. Seeing him standing in her door, unhurt, pissed her off to a roaring level ten. He had just scared the crap out of her. Jumping out, she punched him as hard as she could in the stomach feeling a wicked satisfaction when she heard him grunt. "What were you thinking? I could have killed you!"

"I'm a vampire, remember?" he stated with a sloppy grin, rubbing his stomach. That had actually hurt a little.

"That doesn't mean I couldn't have run over you." She slapped him in the chest. Twice. Hard. Shaking her hurting hand, she glared at him. "You scared the crap out of me."

"You think that's scary?" He leaned in her face with a glare, then grabbed her hand and rubbed it gently. "That's nothing compared to what could be coming after you."

"I'm-" she cleared her throat, looking at his large hands rubbing hers. Just that small touch made her skin crawl in a good wicked way. Okay, Nicole, get a grip. Lifting her eyes to his, she pulled her hand away. "I'm not leaving my home and job. I'll be careful."

Damon nodded, turned away and reached in her car taking the keys out of the ignition. "You have to be the most hard headed, stubborn human I have ever met and believe me I've met a lot of them." Grabbing her elbow, he headed back to the warehouse.

"Hey..." Nicole straightened her legs trying to stop, but she slid right along behind him in the gravel. "What're you doing? Give me my keys, dammit!"

"Stop or you're going to hurt yourself." Damon slowed, but still pulled her along. When she didn't start walking, but kept skidding along the graveled parking lot, he stooped, hitting her in the stomach with his shoulder, lifting her off the ground.

"Put me the fuck down!" Nicole grunted as her soft stomach bounced on his shoulder.

He whacked her butt. "Watch your mouth."

Sucking in her breath, Nicole snarled. "You did not just spank me."

"I'll do it again if you don't watch your language." His grin was downright wicked, and secretly, he hoped she did so he could have a reason to put his hand back on that nice rounded ass.

Knowing he would, she bit her bottom lip to keep her mouth shut. As she bounced up and down, her eyes fell on his rear end that was temptingly close to her face. It would serve him right if she took a bite. God, it was so tempting.

"Don't even think about it," Damon warned as he opened the door to the warehouse, and then set her down. "I bite back." Damon rumbled his voice heavy.

Nicole swayed as the blood rushed to her head. "You're pushing it buddy," She poked his chest with each word.

"And you owe a dollar to the jar," Damon reminded her with a smirk.

Nicole shot him a nasty glare. She hardly ever said the f-word, but he had her so twisted, she didn't know what she was doing anymore.

Mitch, Duncan and Jared stood staring at them with grins on their faces. "I told you he could change her mind," Jared grinned. "He has a way with women."

"I didn't change my mind," Nicole hissed, glaring at Damon. "And he doesn't have a way with me. I am so not like *those* women who probably fall at his feet and follow his every command." Okay...where did that come from?

Jared snorted, trying to hide his grin behind his hand when Damon glared at him. "Shut the hell up, Jared."

Damon turned to Duncan. "As you heard, the human has decided to play Russian roulette with her life, so we need to have someone with her twenty-four-seven until this gets taken care of."

Rolling her eyes, Nicole sighed loud and long. "Come on. This isn't necessary. You guys got better things to do than hang around me, waiting for something that may or may not happen."

"Oh, it's going to happen. Jamison was one of the best and if not for Damon last night, you wouldn't be standing here right now." Jared turned serious. "You'd be dead or wishing you were."

Okay, seeing the funny and goofy Jared turn serious in a blink of an eye put things in perspective. "Okay, so what can I do that doesn't involve me leaving my job and life?"

"Who wants to do it?" Duncan looked between Jared and Damon. Well, the silence said a lot. Nicole felt like an idiot standing there waiting to see who was going to be the sacrifice.

"I'll do it." A man walked out of the shadows of the warehouse.

"What the hell are you doing here?" Damon frowned at the

newcomer.

"I called the council. We need more help down here, so they sent Sid and a few more are on their way." Duncan replied, daring Damon to say anything.

Nicole just stood staring at Sid. Hot damn, these warriors were gorgeous. Not usually attracted to blondes, she had to rethink that one. Standing at the same height as Damon's six-three, he was slimmer, but wasn't hurting for muscles. He looked solid as a rock and actually looked like Brad Pitt starring in a beach boy movie. Ignoring everyone in the warehouse, he stopped in front of Nicole. "Name's Sid Sinclair." He put his hand out and she took it in a strong shake.

She nodded trying not to stare, failing miserably. "Nicole Callahan."

"So you're the children's hero, huh?" Sid dropped her hand and smiled, looking her up and down. "Not much to ya. Figured you'd be ah....taller." he winked.

"Children's hero?" Mitch looked around confused.

"Oh yeah...this woman is well known around the council." Sid smirked at Damon's frown. "She's put a dent in the blood selling business by pulling kids from the homes that are exploiting them."

"Seriously?" Pride warming her, Nicole grinned. All her hard work was finally paying off, and she loved it.

"Oh, yeah," Sid grinned, looking her up and down. "So, I would be honored to guard that body."

Even though Nicole thought Sid was hot, he was not her kind of hot. The vampire growling with a nasty sneer at Sid was more her style. Too bad he was taken.

Duncan knew if he didn't step in, there was going to be a killing. He didn't know why Damon hadn't stepped up, but he knew Damon well enough to know there was a good reason why he didn't. "Sid, I have something else in mind for you. Jared, get your stuff together and go with Nicole."

Jared nodded. He didn't volunteer earlier because he knew something was going on with Damon and Nicole, but hell, Damon hadn't stepped up. "Sure thing." He turned and walked away.

Grabbing his bag, Jared turned to go back out and came face to face with Damon. "Hey, big guy."

"Keep her safe," Damon demanded blocking the door.

"I know my job, Damon. What I don't know is why you aren't doing it."

"I have my reasons."

"Yeah, well hope you can live with them if something happens to her." Jared tried to walk around him.

"Nothing better happen to her Jared, because if it does, it will be your ass," Damon snarled.

Jared dropped his bag and got in Damon's face. "You need to back the fuck off. You don't want to be the one to guard her, so shut the hell up. I don't know what crawled up your ass, but I will guard her and I will die for her if need be. Can you say the same?"

Looking away, Damon backed off. "Get out of here."

"No problem." Jared grabbed his bag. "I don't get you man. I really don't. A blind man can see you have feelings for Nicole and she sure as hell has feelings for you. I never figured you for a coward."

"You don't know what you're talking about." Damon still didn't look at him. But Jared was right, he was a coward. This little human scared the hell out of him.

Shaking his head, Jared walked out. "Whatever."

Chapter 7

The week had gone by in a flash of work, shopping for a dress and missing Damon. Nicole stood in front of her full length mirror making sure her finishing touches for that night's charity dance were acceptable. Jared had taken her and Pam dress shopping earlier in the week and had actually been surprisingly helpful. He had sat patiently as they tried on far too dresses and had even taken the time to comment on each. He actually had very good taste.

Nicole had finally settled on a black chiffon spaghetti strap gown with a sweetheart bodice. It hung with an uneven hem and flowed around to a short train. She had really liked the dress, but had thought it was too casual for the event. Jared, however, had insisted it was perfect. Now looking at her reflection, she was glad she had bought it.

Glancing down at her shoes, she smiled. They were very pretty, but something she wouldn't have bought herself. Once again, Jared had insisted, saying that they set the dress off. They were black satin, with a wraparound instep, rhinestone toe straps and ended with a five-inch stiletto heel. She prayed she didn't break her neck. Glancing one last time in the mirror, she smiled wondering if Damon would be there tonight. For once she looked like a lady, and secretly she wanted him to see her. Jared had warned her not to go anywhere without him tonight. They were afraid that with the combination of public exposure and the prominent people attending the event, it would be a prime time for someone to make a hit on her. Taking a long deep breathe as she pushed her thoughts of Damon and a possible hit aside, she walked out of her bedroom, and closed the door softly behind her.

Jared whistled. "You are absolutely gorgeous."

Nicole blushed. "If you think your flattery will get you more of my fried chicken...you're absolutely right," she laughed and took the arm he offered. "You look very handsome yourself, sir."

"Let's get you to the ball Cinderella," Jared grinned. If this didn't open Damon's eyes, then nothing would. As far as he was concerned,

Nicole was 100% available. Well, that was the way he intended to play it. Jared's grin took a wicked turn as he contemplated his friend's reaction.

Damon tugged at his collar for the hundredth time. God, he hated tuxes, feeling more at home in his BDU's and t-shirts. Everyone was on alert knowing that this would be the best time for someone to make a hit on Nicole. She would be accepting an award tonight for her work with the kids. Yeah, that would make this the best possible time to prove a point. Damon casually looked around at the happy party goers, his hands in his pockets. Where the hell were Jared and Nicole? Pam and her date had arrived a half an hour ago. His nostrils flared thinking of Jared as Nicole's date. Well, he certainly had pushed that into happening, now hadn't he?

"Penny for your thoughts."

Damon looked over at Sid, who sidled up next to him. It looked like he went to the same tux rental place that he had gone to. "Not in the mood, Sid."

"Testy much?" Sid chuckled. "Let's see if I can guess those thoughts and save me a penny. You're beating yourself up for putting the lovely Nicole in the clutches of Jared, who could charm a virginal nun out of her godly habit?"

Damon rolled his eyes, but was surprised that Sid had hit it right on the head. "Not even close," he totally lied.

"Really? Hummm..." Sid winked at a beautiful woman who eyed him as she walked by. "I guess I'm also wrong about the reason Jared is the one with Nicole and not you. I mean she is just a lowly human and not good enough for you. My God, we are of a warrior class and cannot have a human mate. Fates be damned that should happen."

Damon rubbed the bridge of his nose. "I really think it would piss Duncan off if I mopped the floor with your bloody corpse, so why don't you just stop talking and walk away Sid."

Chuckling, Sid patted him on the back. "You know Damon, that's what I have always respected about you. You never were afraid to speak your mind. But you forget, I can read minds too, and lately you have been like a movie of the week. Haven't been blocking very well and that, my friend, is a very dangerous thing in our line of work." Taking a swig of beer, Sid looked around. "We can't choose who we're mated to Damon, so why don't you stop fighting it and go with the flow? Work it out with her that is, after seeing my handsome puss, she still wants you. I can read her mind, but I would bet my last dollar you can't."

Damon watched Sid walk away with his confident swagger, sliding up to the beauty he was eying earlier. Sighing, Damon turned to leave when shock stopped him cold. Jared had just walked in with the most beautiful woman he had ever seen. "Jesus," he groaned realizing it was Nicole like he had never seen her before. Gone were her jeans and t-shirts, and in place was a gown that was tight in all the right places and flowed in all the others. Her pale blonde hair had been left loose with the sides tied up into a jeweled comb in the back. Soft wisps of hair framed her face. From the top of her lovely head, to the bottom of her high heeled shoes, she was perfect. And all the instincts that drove his kind to their mates screamed "MINE".

"Now that my friend is one hot piece of ..." Sid had stepped back to his side, staring at Nicole.

"If you want to keep those fangs, don't finish that sentence."

"Then do something about it and do it soon, cause if you pass on that, I sure as hell won't." Sid chuckled moving out of the way when Damon went to grab him.

Jared and Nicole made their way to Damon after being stopped a few times. Nicole's gaze kept flicking to him. She had never seen anyone so handsome. His hair was tied back and the tux looked like it was made for his fine hard body. In this room full of people, she had never felt more alone in her life. She knew next to nothing about this man, yet every fiber of her being wanted him. Needed him.

"Have you already talked to Duncan?" Damon asked Jared, dragging his eyes from Nicole.

Feeling Nicole's hurt rolling off her in waves, Jared seriously wanted to punch Damon in the face. What an idiot. "Yeah, I know what's up." Jared took Nicole's hand giving it a squeeze and moved past him heading toward their table. He knew for a fact that Nicole had dressed for Damon tonight, even if she would slit her own throat before admitting it and Damon had pretty much thrown it back in her face by ignoring her.

Not looking at Damon in fear he would see the hurt in her eyes, she let Jared lead her away; the hurt starting to turn toward anger. She knew she wasn't as beautiful as the woman he was with at the warehouse, but he didn't have to act like she was nothing. He wouldn't even acknowledge her and that hurt. Determined to enjoy the rest of the evening, she sat down in the chair Jared pulled out for her and smiled up at him.

"He's an idiot," Jared frowned as she sat down beside her.

Nicole laughed, "No, he's not." Shaking her head, she put her hand on his shoulder. "Thanks for everything, Jared. Don't be mad at Damon. He's your friend, and I'm a big girl with a little crush." There, she admitted it. That was the first step to getting over this awful obsession with a vampire she didn't really know.

As the night went on, Nicole really did enjoy herself. Along at the table with her and Jared were Mitch, Pam and her date Kenny. Soon the dinner was over and the speeches began. The last to get up was Mitch. Nicole suddenly developed a case of nerves as Mitch began to talk, afraid of what he might say. Lord knew when Mitch got on a roll no one was safe.

Mitch took the podium with a huge smile on his face. He told a few jokes to break the ice, then smiled down at Nicole. "Tonight I have the great pleasure of presenting the Community Service Award to one of my employees. When Nicole Callahan first walked into my office intent on getting the job she was applying for, I knew I'd hit pay dirt.

She was the most optimistic person I had ever met, and after experiencing the daily life of a social service employee, she remains just as optimistic, if not more so. I am very lucky to have a full staff of employees who are good at their jobs day in and day out, but Nicole has always gone a step above what is expected because she has been where these kids are coming from and what they are going through, being a ward of the state herself for the first 18 years of her life. Her story is one that she freely relays to the kids she deals with, so they know she truly does understand, but that is not my story to tell. I will tell you, however, if there is anyone who deserves this award, it is Nicole. On top of her day job with us, which believe me can often be twenty-four-seven, she volunteers at the Free Store, homeless shelters, women's centers, Children's Hospital, and The Boys and Girls Club. Also, beware, because I know she is actively recruiting volunteers for the softball charity game coming up." Everyone laughed, and Mitch grinned, liking the attention. "But the most important job she does is taking children, who have no safe place, no home and nobody to care for them and placing them in homes, so they have a place to grow up safely."

Stunned, Nicole sat gaping at Mitch. She figured Mitch would treat this like a roast, and savor every moment of telling the room how big of a pain in his butt she was, alongside a little bit of niceness for good measure. But this was not what she expected at all.

When Mitch turned his attention to her with a slightly crooked grin, she considered that she may have thought too soon.

"I would like to present this plaque to you, Nicole Callahan, and personally tell you, thank you for your hard work and dedication. It has been inspiring, even to a mean, grumpy boss like me." Everyone clapped loudly as Mitch held the plaque toward her.

Nicole stood, grinning from ear to ear. Jared took her hand and led her to the podium, giving her his arm while walking her up the steps before returning to his seat. Looking up at Mitch, she took the plaque with a smile and tears.

"Didn't see that coming did you Callahan?" He leaned down and kissed her cheek. "You deserve it."

Nicole laughed, "Thank you, Mitch." She kissed his cheek back.

He looked embarrassed, but before leaving he added. "Yeah, well don't get used to it, cause Monday it's back to normal."

Shaking her head grinning, she watched him trot down the steps, leaving her alone in front of a hundred people, who were all staring at her waiting for her to say something. Clearing her throat, she looked over the crowd. "Ever since I can remember, I wanted to be a social worker helping children. Even from a young age I knew the exact title because that is who I pretty much grew up with. I was never adopted, and I can't say that I'm bitter about that because being in foster home after foster home gave me what I needed to become a good social worker for the kids. To me, this is not my job, but my life. I love what I do and believe me it's not for the paycheck." She grinned at Mitch when everyone whooped and laughter filled the room.

"Seriously, if I didn't have bills and need to eat, I would do this for the satisfaction I get from it. To be honest, I think anyone who does something for the betterment of children should get this award, so I share this with all my co-workers who put their lives on hold for the children who are not so fortunate. Thank you so much for changing our children's futures, their lives, and giving them hope." With a smile, she began to walk away from the podium, but stopped and went back. "Oh, and please, I really do need volunteers for the softball game, so see me. I got the sign-up sheet with me." Nicole waved the sheet with a grin.

The room erupted with laughter and applause as Jared helped her back to her seat, but not before he hugged her placing a quick peck on the lips. When her eyes shot to his in surprise, he winked.

Damon had watched every guy in the place dance with Nicole and it was driving him nearly insane. So far no attempt had been made on her life. Warriors were scattered everywhere. If anyone made a move toward her, they would be on them. Even when she danced, Jared was right there ready. When the band announced that the last dance was to be played, Damon made his move.

Pam stood talking to Nicole and Jared as Damon walked up. "Will you dance with me?" He held his hand out.

Looking up at him, her heart thumped so loudly, she was sure everyone could hear it. Nodding, she put her hand in his as he led her to the dance floor. Yeah, like she could say no to him. Not a chance. Every man she had danced with tonight, she'd wanted it to be him.

A few couples had taken advantage of the final dance and were scattered about the dance floor. Pulling her into his arms, Damon didn't say a word. He just held her tightly, swaying with the music. When the song ended, she wanted to plead for one more song, but the lights came up and it was over. With a sigh, she pulled away and looked up into his golden eyes.

"Thank you for the dance." His voice was low and sent shivers down her body, as his voice caressed her skin.

Not trusting herself to speak, she smiled and nodded. Turning, she looked for Jared before she made a complete fool of herself and begged him for one night. God, she was a fool.

"We need to talk," Damon spoke before she could make her break from him.

"I don't think that's a good idea." Nicole really didn't think it was a good idea. As much as she wanted him to want her, she couldn't get the other woman out of her head. She didn't break up relationships, and there was no way she could compete with that woman.

Damon watched her walk away from him to Jared. When Jared smiled down at her and draped his arm across her shoulder, Damon felt a deep seated fear that he might be too late. The fear turned deadly when Jared leaned down and whispered something in Nicole's ear, making her laugh. Damon headed toward them.

Grabbing Jared's arm, he pulled it off of Nicole's shoulder. "I have this," Damon growled at Jared grabbing her hand, pulling her away.

"What are you doing?" Nicole gasped.

Damon eyed her as he pulled her toward a private corner. "I said we need to talk."

"And I said that wasn't a good idea." Nicole glanced around, but thankfully no one seemed to be paying attention.

"Why the hell not?" Damon asked, giving Jared a death stare when he noticed him walking toward them. "What, you want Jared now? Is that how it is?"

Nicole's eyes popped open wide, her head snapping back. "Seriously?" When she saw that he was serious, she got close to him with a death stare of her own. "*Go to hell,*" she hissed as quietly as she could without drawing attention.

The crowd had thinned out and only a few remained moving toward the door to leave. Nicole and Damon stood glaring at each other. "Answer me."

Rolling her eyes, she threw her hands up. "Sure. Yeah. Me and Jared are hot and heavy. Don't know why that should bother you when you have a gorgeous girlfriend, which by the way you should get back to. I'm sure she's waiting for you."

"Girlfriend?" This time, she freed herself and walked out the door with Jared, his damn arm around her shoulder again. God, he was going to kill the son of a bitch. With one last glance he headed toward the back exit. "Girlfriend?" He repeated, stumped. A couple of stragglers passed by eyeing him warily.

"You okay?" Jared looked down at her frowning.

"Yeah, I'm good," Nicole lied with a smile. "Thanks for coming with me, even though it was your job."

"Best job I've ever had, honey." Jared wiggled his eyebrows.

God, why couldn't she be attracted to Jared instead of Mr. Doom and Gloom. Jared was nice, a real sweetie and very handsome in a dark mysterious kind of way, but he just didn't do it for her. Before she could reply, a motorcycle raced up to them and stopped. Turning to look, she saw Damon straddling a solid black and chrome Harley, sending her heart thumping out of her chest. God, he looked good on the bike. She was a sucker for a man on a Harley.

"Get on," Damon demanded over the roar of the bike, his eyes holding her hostage.

Was he serious? She was in a freakin evening gown. Shaking her head, she turned to Jared. "Please take me home."

Nodding, Jared glanced at Damon. "If you want to talk to her, meet us at her place." He turned and led her away to his car.

"I don't want to talk to him, Jared." Nicole stared at him accusingly.

Once at the car, he turned her to face him as Damon's bike roared past them. Jared watched Damon disappear trying to get a read on him, but he had him blocked. "I can read you, Nicole. I just think you need to hear him out."

"You've been reading my mind?" Nicole was mortified.

"Bits and pieces," he admitted opening the car door for her. "But don't worry. I don't gab." Before closing the door, he gave her a wink.

Heat flooded her face. This was so not cool. After he got in and started the car, Nicole turned to look at Jared. "You need to stop doing that Jared." Nicole groaned when he laughed. "Seriously, I don't want you in my head."

"Well, believe me honey, I don't really want to be in there as much as you might think." Pulling out in traffic, he quickly maneuvered the streets to her apartment. "Hearing your every thought about one of my partners in different modes of dress isn't as pleasing to me as it seems to be to you."

"Oh. My. God!" Nicole's hands flew to her face.

Jared laughed, "Listen, you can block anyone from reading your mind."

"How?" Nicole spoke through her hands not ready to uncover her flushed embarrassment. Talk about awkward.

"You can tell if someone is trying to power into your head. First, you'll feel a tingly pressure, a nagging feeling in your head. When you start feeling it, you mentally throw up a wall. Since we all can pretty much read each other, we keep a permanent wall up." Jared cruised up to a stop light. "Believe me, once you know the signs and start doing it, it becomes second nature. Usually, I think of myself naked and boy oh boy do the guys go flying out of my head."

Nicole laughed sliding her hands from her face. "No you don't."

He chuckled. "Go ahead and try," he urged, and then threw a wicked grin her way. "I'll try to get in, and you just think of yourself naked and...."

"Stop it." She smacked his arm shaking her head. Closing her eyes, she concentrated. She loved dogs and always wanted a puppy, but was never able to get one.

"Very good," Jared said after a few minutes. "All I can see are a bunch of puppies. Keep working on it around me, and I'll keep testing you."

They pulled in her parking lot and spotted Damon leaning against his bike waiting. Jared pulled up behind the bike leaving the car running. "Aren't you coming in?"

"Nope. You two need to talk." Jared nodded toward Damon, "Give him a chance, Nicole. As much as he can piss me off, he's one of the good guys and I think you both need alone time."

Nicole watched Damon walk to her side of the car and then took his hand when he offered to help her out. "Thanks Jared...for everything."

"Anytime honey, anytime." Jared pulled away, leaving them alone in the parking lot.

Nerves fluttered in her stomach. "Hey," was the only thing that popped into her head to say.

Staring down, he gave her that sexy crooked grin, "Hey." Grabbing her hand, he led her toward her apartment.

Once they were inside, Nicole didn't know what to do or say. Her apartment felt overcrowded with him in it making it hard for her to breathe. Putting her small bag on the counter, she headed to the fridge and grabbed two beers. Handing one to Damon, she cleared her tight throat, but didn't know what to say, so she twisted her cap off taking a huge gulp.

"Thanks." He followed suit and downed half the bottle. Then he said something that totally blew her mind. "So how have you been?"

"How have I been?" she repeated, eyes widening. Finding out she was a target of killers, having a mind blowing kiss from him, seeing him with one of the most beautiful women Nicole had ever seen a day after the mind blowing kiss, dressing for him and him alone tonight and being totally ignored until the end of the night, and then topping all that off, accusing her of wanting Jared and now he wanted to know how she had been. "Peachy. Just freakin peachy, Damon," Nicole snorted shaking her head in disbelief.

Damon finished his beer in one more long swallow and set the bottle down. "Listen Nicole..."

Shaking her head, she set her bottle down next to his, hers unfinished.

She needed to keep her head around him. No way did she need to get drunk. "No, you listen Damon. I'm not going to be that woman."

Looking slightly puzzled, Damon asked, "What woman?"

"I am not competing with that woman." Nicole reached up, unpinning her hair, missing the flare of heat blazing in Damon's golden eyes as she massaged her aching scalp. "As if I could even begin to compete with a woman like that."

Damon was ready to explode in frustration. "I have no idea what you're talking about, Nicole."

"*The woman*, Damon," Nicole huffed, already tired of the conversation. "The woman at the gym you were with. I don't break up relationships and I can't imagine you'd want to end a relationship with someone like her. I didn't mean to kiss you that night. I guess it was all the excitement that happened. I had no idea you were attached. You don't need to apologize for the kiss. It was my fault. It was no big deal." God, she was rambling. Realizing that fact, she sucked her lips between her teeth hoping that would help shut her big mouth.

Damon was shocked to say the least. Girlfriend, apologize, and the kiss not being a big fucking deal. He shook his head as if to clear it of her constant blabbing. He took a step closer to her. "First of all I was not going to apologize for kissing you, second of all I don't have a girlfriend and thirdly, if it wasn't a big deal, then I obviously didn't do it right." His face was inches from hers, practically nose to nose.

"Oh..." Good one Nicole, she told herself. "Well, ah, I just wanted to let you know that you're off the hook. I'm not some chick who thinks a kiss is a proposal or something, and I didn't want to make waves with your girlfriend."

"I told you I didn't have a girlfriend." Damon put both hands on the wall he had slowly backed her up against, caging her in with his massive arms. "If I had a girlfriend, I would not have kissed you."

God he smelled so good, Nicole thought, taking a deep breath. She could hardly think straight with him so close. "I just assumed the woman was your girlfriend, at least it looked that way." Okay, she had to get away from him, but dammit, she kept leaning closer. "So, as I said, I didn't want to cause problems, so I'm sorry. She is really beautiful and you guys look great together. Kind of like Ken and Barbie great." Okay, she was rambling again.

Understanding flashed in his eyes, and that sexy grin spread across his face. She was jealous. "She's a donor." Damon chuckled, "Not my girlfriend."

"A donor?" Nicole wondered if she really wanted to know what the knock out red head donated.

Damon leaned back and rubbed his hand down his face. "I'm a vampire Nicole. I need blood. She is a paid donor, hired by the council."

"Are you kidding me?" Nicole was amazed. "You mean I could apply for a job as a blood donor?"

Okay, his blood just shot up a few degrees as did his cock at the thought of tasting her blood. Shaking his head, he changed the subject fast. "Are you and Jared involved?"

"No." Nicole stared up into his eyes.

"You and red aren't involved?"

"No." Damon answered her right back, point blank without blinking.

"Then why have you been acting like you don't want to have anything to do with me? I mean, after we kissed you would hardly look at me." She really tried to keep the hurt out of her voice. She failed. It had hurt...a lot.

"Truth?" When she nodded, he pushed his body closer leaning his head down, his lips mere inches from her ear. Goose bumps pimpled her skin. "Because I have never wanted anyone the way I want you. I can't promise you anything, Nicole. Just tonight. I can just promise you tonight."

Nicole inhaled his scent deeply and with his body so close and his confession spoken so softly, she decided she would take what he could give. Deep inside, she knew that wasn't going to be enough for her and it would be her heart breaking in the end, but she had never depended on more than the present from anyone before, so why should it be different with him. Making a decision she knew would change her life, she lifted her hand and ran a finger across his full lips. "I want tonight with you, Damon."

With a sexy moan, he dropped his fingers to the front of her dress and gently brushed against her breasts, cupping the soft mounds in his hand. He took his time, exploring each breast slowly, first one and then the other, massaging with intimate authority. "You are so beautiful."

Nicole's head fell back, and she moaned softly. He pushed the straps of her dress off her shoulders and drew in a sharp breath as the gentle curves of her skin were exposed to his hungry gaze. "Damon." Her voice came out husky and slow, like that of a temptress, surprising even to her own ears. She didn't know where the sound had come from, but his response was instantaneous - his thick erection rising, pressing against her stomach. He made no effort to conceal his arousal, grinding his hips in a slow circle, pressing firmly against her.

Wasting no time at all, he pushed the straps further down her shoulders; the gown fell to her waist, caught by the swell of her hips, both her shoulders and breasts exposed. He groaned when her nipples came out of the silk. Bending his head to blow hot air over the erect peaks, he gently circled one then the other with his tongue. "I have been dying to know what you taste like."

Nicole arched into him reveling in the sensations. She couldn't help herself...and she didn't want to. Her breasts felt incredibly heavy, the tips beginning to tingle, the mounds beginning to ache. She moaned when he tugged at a nipple with his teeth, flicked the sensitive bud with his tongue, and then took the entire tip vigorously into his mouth. The sensual heat engulfed her like a fire as his hands cupped, his fingers massaged, and his mouth sucked hotly. She clutched a fistful of beautiful blue-black hair, bringing him even closer. His mouth was creating an inferno between her legs, jolts of electricity sizzling through her body and cresting at the apex between her thighs. He was turning her core to liquid fire as he feasted on her breasts.

Moving down her body, his tongue burned a path to her belly button, dipping in and out before traveling just above where the dress stopped. Hooking his thumbs in the material, it took every amount of self-control he had not to rip it from her body, from his prize. He stood back up, his lips inches from hers. "Are you sure about this because once this dress comes off..." He glanced down at her bared breasts, his golden eyes almost black. "I won't be able to stop."

Placing both of her hands on his face, she brought his gaze to her. "I'm sure," her husky whisper was all it took. He took her mouth in a kiss that was tender, yet commanding, claiming her with each sensual swipe of his tongue.

When he pulled back, there was something in his gaze, something stark and primitive and wild being unleashed; a fierce hunger...for her and that alone set her blood on fire. Never had a man looked at her with such intensity. God, this was such a mistake because with a certainty that scared her, no other man would ever compare to Damon...no moment would ever live up to this one, but even as it was the biggest mistake of her life, it was going to be the best, mind blowing mistake she'd ever make.

Pressing his hard sex shamelessly against her, she felt the gentle scraping of his fangs against her neck, the soft graze of two sharp edges moving lightly over her throat. He nibbled once, bit at her skin, and then he quickly pulled away...even as she relaxed into him. She found herself kissing the hollow of his throat, her hands reaching down to unbutton his shirt eager to feel skin to skin. He shrugged out of his shirt, exposing a rock-hard chest with astonishing definition, and as her eyes dropped lower, her breath caught in her throat, he had a sinfully gorgeous six-pack, row after row of flawless abdominal muscles rippling beneath smooth skin on a hairless, flat stomach.

Again, he held her gaze for a fraction of a second, although it felt like an eternity. When he next took her mouth with his, she could taste the increasing intensity of his need. His shaft jerked against her stomach. His hands reached down, pushing the dress from her hips, sending it to the floor as he cupped her bottom pulling her tightly against him. Nicole melted into his hard frame, lifting her leg to wrap it around his powerful thigh. She offered up her body. She strained and arched into him wanting more, needing more. She rubbed the uncomfortable heat between her legs over his hamstring as he stroked and explored her body.

He kissed her with far more demand, while nipping at her bottom lip and swirling his tongue around hers. He tasted every part of her mouth with a growing, insistent hunger. With one hand still grasping her waist, he reached down to remove his pants, freeing his rigid length. Nicole caught her breath at the sight of his enormous arousal, now standing at full attention. He was pressed painfully against her belly, his sex, positively magnificent, smooth as silk, yet hard as steel, an erotic promise of ecstasy just waiting to be thrust into her welcoming body.

She gasped as he ripped the pair of thin silk panties off her. "I'll buy you a new pair," he growled, causing her sex to throb with rising need.

He inserted a finger then, deep into her hot, wet sheath, and began to gently knead the tight, soft folds, drawing liquid heat from her. "God, you're so wet." A soft moan escaped her lips as she felt him insert a second finger, and then a third: stretching her, caressing her, stabbing deep in an erotic effort to push her over the edge and get her ready for him. Nicole couldn't stand it any longer. She fractured into a thousand pieces, her body trembling in violent waves of pleasure as the powerful orgasm shook her. She cried out, fisting her hands in his hair, tears streaming down her face at the power of her release. She felt completely exposed - vulnerable - entirely open to his command. "You are beautiful."

He lifted her as if she weighed nothing, taking her to her room, and laid her gently on the bed. He grasped her thighs with his strong, firm hands and knelt between her legs, gently easing them apart. And then he took the length of his rigid, sex into his hand and pressed the head against her core. His erection felt enormous against her entrance—so much so that Nicole wondered if she would be able to take all of him inside her. But she wanted him. All of him. A low, throaty hiss escaped his lips as he thrust forward into her tight, hot sheath, stretching her with the heavy width of his sex. It had been years since she'd been with anyone and even then it was only twice. She started to moan as her body stretched to accommodate his size, her hands pushing against the muscular wall of his chest in an automatic response to the slight burning sensation of his dominant entry.

Damon started to pull away, concern shadowing his eyes. "No...please." Nicole cried out. "I'm fine."

Damon took her hands from his chest and held them down above her head, pinning both arms gently in one strong hand. "Relax." He bent to taste her breasts again, easing up on the pressure while her body adjusted to his size. "That's it, honey, you were made for me...you can take more," he groaned in sheer ecstasy when her body finally accepted the full length of him, and her answering groan told him all she couldn't say. Together, they slowly began to move in unison, her hips rising to meet his every thrust, his hard, flat pelvis lingering and rotating against her cleft to heighten her pleasure. "You feel so...damn...good." Nicole reached up to cup his face and the rhythm picked up. Damon continued to bury himself deep inside of her, pulling back almost to the point of withdrawal only to thrust forward again and again, until the passion grew so intense between them he could no longer restrain his need. He began to plunge harder...faster...each stroke more urgent, more possessive than the last.

Nicole clutched at his shoulders, dug her fingernails into his back. She cried out, raising her hips to meet his...writhing beneath him. She took all he could give her and wanted even more...would always want more.

Damon felt her release and his soon followed. His body stilled savoring the last tremors of her body against his, his head buried in the crook of her neck, breathing her scent in and stopping short of biting her sweet neck arched for the taking. Knowing if he didn't get away, he would do just that. He pushed himself up and away from her.

Not really knowing what to do or say, Nicole had a sudden fit of nerves and embarrassment. Pulling the sheet over her body, she glanced at Damon under lowered lashes to see his reaction to what they had just shared. She needed to say something instead of sitting here like some pitiful virgin waiting for words of love and worship. God, she was pathetic. "You hungry?" Her voice squeaked. Clearing her throat, she asked again. "You hungry?"

She had no idea just how hungry he was. Nodding his head, he looked toward the bathroom. "You mind if I take a shower?"

"No, go ahead." Nicole wrapped the sheet around her and stood up. "Towels are in the closet by the bathroom door."

He nodded. "Thanks."

Nicole hated this awkwardness toward each other. She just had the best sex that she had ever had, and she was not going to ruin the chance of it not happening again. "Damon," she called out before he shut the door. He turned; his expression unreadable. "I just had the best freakin sex of my life. Let's not ruin it by awkward moments. I'm not expecting marriage or I love yous, okay. Let's just call this a friends with benefits arrangement and go from there. What do ya say...buddy?" She laughed lightly when he just stood there staring at her.

Stalking back into the room, he slammed the door shut and prowled toward her. Grabbing her up by the waist, he pinned her to the wall as she wrapped her legs around him. "I wish I could give you more," he growled in her ear before plunging his hard length into her for a second time. "You deserve more."

87

Nicole was too lost in the feeling of the moment, too lost in Damon and too afraid to answer.

Chapter 8

"Friends with benefits?" Pam gasped in mock horror. "You slut!"

"Shut up, Pam." Nicole threw a small paperweight that had been sitting on her desk at Pam.

"So, you're telling me that you can do the friends with benefits deal without getting your heart involved?" Pam asked in disbelief as she placed the paperweight back on Nicole's desk.

"Yes," Nicole nodded shuffling papers around on her desk, refusing to look at Pam in fear that she'd give herself away. She could do this dammit. She was an adult and could have a wickedly delightful affair with one hot vampire. People did it every day, all over the world, so why couldn't she, dammit.

"I call bullshit Nicole," Pam snorted leaning back in her chair, eyeing Nicole and shaking her head. "You have the biggest, most open heart I have ever seen. You give so much of yourself, never asking for anything. I have seen the way you look at Damon, and I would bet my bony butt, you're halfway in love with him already."

Nicole's stomach felt hollow as she sat listening to Pam knowing she was right, but determined that she could handle it. "I don't even know him that well Pam. I mean, come on, give me a break. Have you never had hot monkey sex with someone without a proposal of everlasting love and all that crap?"

Eyes popping wide, Pam laughed out so loud, it sounded more like a scream. Suddenly, Nicole's small office was filled with vampire as they burst into the room, guns drawn. Both women screamed, Pam falling out of her chair. After her initial shock, Nicole slapped her hand across her mouth laughing uncontrollably.

"What is it!?" Jared's eyes roamed the room, looking for trouble.

Picking herself up from the floor, Pam looked at Nicole, more laughter bubbled up. "Girl talk."

"Girl talk?" Jared shouted in disbelief. "Jesus, we thought someone was being killed. We heard a scream."

"Actually, that was me laughing," Pam snorted. "Sorry, but it was her fault."

Putting their weapons away, Jared rolled his eyes at Damon. "Girl talk." He turned to walk out of the room disgusted. "Next time you have a girl talk, warn us if there's going to be screaming please. Scared the shit out of me."

Damon glanced at Nicole. "You okay?" His eyes lowered half-mast making him look sexy as hell.

"Dandy," Nicole smiled, her stomach flip flopping all over the place.

He turned to leave, but before he did, a wicked grin tipped his lips and he left with a wink.

"Yep, you're a goner," Pam sighed shaking her head at Nicole's dewy eyed stare following Damon out the door.

"Shut up, Pam before I throw something heavier than that paperweight."

After venting about her sexcapades, it was time to get serious and work. "Where to?" Damon got behind the wheel glancing at her. He absolutely refused to step foot in her car and demanded that he drive. Nicole agreed without any argument since her car was on its last wheel.

Nicole gave him the address and watched him input it into his GPS wondering if Mitch would splurge for one. It sure would come in handy with all the places she had to go. Maybe she would catch him in a good mood one day. Yeah, right.

"What were you guys talking about with Mitch?" Nicole asked as he pulled onto the highway. When she had her caseload packed up, she had gone looking for him so they could get going. She had found him and Jared in Mitch's office.

"Better security at your offices." Damon checked his review mirror merging into traffic. "Even when this is over, the security should be better. As many people as you piss off on a daily basis, they need better security."

Nicole rolled her eyes. "What did he say?" She didn't piss that many people off and certainly not on a daily basis.

"He agreed and is going to let our team head it up."

Well, there went the GPS. "Do you really think that's necessary?" Since the club incident, there hadn't been any attempts on her life or even a hint that anyone wanted her dead.

"Yeah, I do." Damon eyed her. "Just because nothing has happened doesn't mean they gave up. These people don't give up, Nicole. Not by a long shot."

"Well, aren't you Sally sunshine," Nicole snorted. "It's the third house on the right."

"You need to take this more serious." Damon followed her up to the door, his gaze landing on the sexy sway of her hips. Yeah, listen to who's talking. They were talking about her life, and he couldn't take his eyes off her curvy ass.

"I am taking it seriously. I just don't like having my life dictated to me." Knocking on the door, Nicole peeked back catching him looking at her ass. Heat flared through her body. She had never experienced a man like Damon paying attention to her in any way, let alone checking out her ass and damn, wasn't that a turn on.

His eyes rising to hers, he stepped up onto the porch beside her. "Better dictated to than dead."

Before she could respond, the door swung open showing a six year old vampire jumping up and down clapping his hands. "Nicki...Nicki..." he shouted, laughing in delight, tiny fangs dipping below his upper lip.

"Hey there, Munchkin," Nicole tapped him on the nose. "Where's your mom and dad?"

"Goodness, Austin." His mom came up smiling. "Calm down and let them in."

Austin took off running around the house calling Nicole's name, sending the dog running for cover.

"Well, he sure looks happy, Betty," Nicole chuckled as she stepped inside, Damon close on her heels.

"We all are, thanks to you." Betty Rawlins smiled, her eyes bright with tears.

Uncomfortable with the praise, she turned to Damon. "Betty, this is Damon DeMasters. He's helping out on some of our cases, so he's riding along with me today."

Damon stuck out his hand and took Betty's hand in a gentle grasp. "It's nice to meet you Ma'am," Damon smiled stepping back.

"Lord, call me Betty," she giggled blushing. "Look at me keeping you all standing in the doorway. Come in and have a seat."

Nicole grinned knowing Damon probably had that effect on all the women he came in contact with. He sure had with her and still did. "So how are things going, Betty?" Nicole looked around with a keen eye seeing a well-kept home. Nothing raised red flags. Austin was now chasing the dog around.

"They couldn't be better, Nicole." Betty lead them to the kitchen table where they all sat down. "Greg got the promotion at work he's been working so hard for, and I gave my two weeks' notice so I could spend more time with Austin. They didn't have any part-time work, so I already have a job set up that will allow me to be home when Austin is out of school."

Nicole had pulled their file from her briefcase setting it on the table. "That's wonderful Betty. How is Austin adjusting to school?" Nicole wrote a few notes.

"Like a fish to water. He gets along well with the other kids and is doing well in his school work. The teacher has nothing but good things to say about him," Betty beamed like a proud parent.

Nicole made a few more notes then turned looking for Austin. "Hey Munchkin, want to take me to check out your room?"

Austin jumped from where he was playing with the dog. "Yep." He ran over grabbing her hand, and pulled her along behind him, talking a mile a minute.

"He sure loves Nicole," Betty smiled watching them disappear into his room. "We owe her so much."

Damon also watched them disappear before turning his attention back to the woman seated across from him. "May I ask you a question?"

"Sure, but first would you like something to drink?" Betty offered.

"No thank you. I'm fine," he smiled. "My question is a little personal, so if you don't want to answer, that's fine."

"Mr. DeMasters..."

"Damon."

She blushed again, "Damon, my husband and I have been asked so many personal questions since we decided to adopt, that I seriously doubt you've come up with one we haven't heard."

"Yes, I guess you have, especially if Nicole has been on your case from the beginning," Damon chuckled.

"I see you know her well. Yes, she has been our case manager from the beginning and it's been a pleasure." Betty chuckled, "I remember once having to call her at three in the morning because Austin was throwing up constantly and we didn't know what was wrong. I mean all kids get sick, but we didn't have any understanding about vampire children. We didn't think they could or would get sick. Nicole came right over and sat up with us until he was feeling better. We still don't know what it was, but she thought it could have been a side effect from being turned."

"That could be, but the truth of it is, this is even new to us. I have lived a long time and have only now been around vampire children since we cannot have them, they can only be turned." Damon glanced back toward the room Nicole had disappeared into. "What made you decide to adopt a vampire child?"

"To be honest, we were against it." Betty glanced up at him hesitant, "I mean who in their right might would want to adopt a child who would always be six years old. A year ago, your kind didn't exist to us. When we first met with Nicole, we never dreamed of adopting a vampire and she didn't ask. Instead, she gave us files on children she felt would fit well with us. Little did we know there were human and vampire children in the files she gave us. We picked two we wanted to meet with and Austin was one of them. As soon as I laid eyes on him, I was in love and so was my husband."

"And when you found out he was a vampire?" Damon asked beyond curious.

Betty shrugged her shoulders and smiled with love, "It didn't matter. I saw him playing in a room full of kids, he looked up and came walking over to me and my husband. As big as you please, he grinned the biggest grin I had ever seen showing his little fangs, grabbed my hand and said, 'I'm Austin. You want to see my toys?' and that was it for me."

He could hear Nicole's husky laughter coming from Austin's room. "It seems he's very lucky to have found someone like you and your husband."

"We're the lucky ones." Betty glanced back at the room hearing more giggling. "Nicole has set us up with someone to help us understand more about your race, and we've learned so much. I now understand that even though Austin will always look six years old, his mentality will mature as he ages. It is just so cruel for someone to do something like this to a child."

Damon nodded and stood when Austin and Nicole came back. "Well Betty, everything looks great here and this little guy is a joy." Nicole gave Austin a high five. "I think we can go to yearly visits from here on out. If you need anything at all, you have all my numbers so don't hesitate to call." Nicole wrapped up her paperwork and put it away.

"We'll never be able to thank you, Nicole." Betty walked over to her and hugged her warmly.

"Just seeing that little guy happy is enough." Nicole picked up her brief case. "Also don't forget to report any unusual activity, such as anyone contacting you about Austin that is not from my office."

"I won't forget." Betty frowned. "That is so awful what people are doing. Using these poor children for their blood just to get a high. Sickening."

"Yes it is," Nicole nodded. "So call me if anyone ever approaches you."

"Better yet," Damon pulled a card out of his back pocket, "reach someone at this number. Tell them my name and tell them I told you to call."

Betty took the card missing Nicole's frown. "I will. Anything to help stop the sickening abuse."

Damon hadn't missed Nicole's frown. After they said their goodbyes, they headed out to the next appointment. Even knowing he was going to catch hell, he couldn't help the admiration he had for her. For someone to care so much about another was rare. For someone to care about a race so different from their own was almost nonexistent, at least in his world.

Chapter 9

To his surprise, Nicole didn't once say anything about him handing his card out to everyone they met with today. Each time she reminded them to contact her if anyone approached them about buying blood. It was a sad conversation to have with new foster parents, but that was the way of their world now. It was pretty much protocol.

The rest of the day went the same as their first meeting with Austin. Each showing great gratitude to Nicole, and the kids absolutely adored her. She showed the vampire children the same respect and kindness as she did the human children. There was no bias.

"Do you need to go back to the office?" Damon asked, breaking the silence of the car.

"No, not really," Nicole sighed. "I'd really love to get something to eat before we go back to my place though. I really don't want to cook."

"What would you like?" Damon slowed for a stop light. "There's seafood, steak, Chinese..."

"Pizza!" She chuckled at his pained look.

"Pizza?" he groaned. "Seriously?"

"You can't tell me you don't like pizza," she teased. "Everybody likes pizza."

"Never had it," he replied pulling into the first pizza joint he saw.

"Oh. My. God." Nicole stared at him like he has just committed the worst heinous crime. "Never?"

He shook his head, "Ever."

Meeting around the front of the car, she grabbed his hand. "Well, you are in for a treat vamp," she grinned leading him inside.

Once at the table, she ordered a large pizza with everything and two draft beers. She thought about ordering three so she could dump the third one on the waitress's head. The woman, more or less, laid herself out on the table offering herself to Damon for an appetizer. She decided it would be a waste of good beer and choose to give the hoe the evil eye instead. Finally, she noticed everyone was staring at Damon. The women with lust and the men with hate and fear. What the hell. Okay, it looked like her evil eye was going to work overtime tonight.

"Don't, Nicole," Damon took a long draw of his beer leaning back in his chair looking relaxed.

"Don't what?" She shot another dude sitting behind Damon a nasty glare. He glanced her way then went back to eating.

"Glare at everyone. I'm used to it." Damon took another swig of his draft. "Not everyone is happy we've made our presence known."

"Yeah, well I'm not used to it and I refuse to let anyone mistreat you in any way," she puffed out her chest and lifted her chin daring him to say anything more on the subject.

Damon grinned at her tough girl attitude, "Yes ma'am."

The waitress brought their pizza asking if there was anything else she could get them, but her eyes never left Damon. "No that's it," Nicole told the waitress with a roll of her eyes. Placing a piece of pizza on a plate, she pushed it toward him. "Time to taste heaven."

Damon looked at the odd food and frowned. That sure as hell didn't look like heaven to him. Glancing up at Nicole, he watched her lift a piece of pizza to her lips taking a large bite, the cheese stringing from her lips to the pizza. Her tongue licked out to wrap around the cheese to bring it back to her mouth. Her moan was one of ecstasy. His pants became uncomfortably tight. Damn if this was the way she ate pizza, he was going to buy the fucking place.

Nicole noticed he wasn't eating, but watching her. "Go on," Nicole urged as she nudged her slice at his. "Eat."

Damon picked it up and eyed it, "Do I have to?"

"Yes," Nicole chuckled shaking her head. "I can't believe you have never had pizza. Go on, don't be a chicken."

Damon took a bite, and then took another showing no reaction at all.

"Well...?" Nicole waited at the edge of her seat. It was so cool watching someone try something for the first time.

Taking a swig of beer, he nodded, "Not bad Callahan. Not bad." He laughed at her frown. "Okay, it's not heaven, but a close runner up." He didn't add that heaven was being inside her, tasting her, seeing her sweet body quivering underneath his and man, if he didn't stop there, he wouldn't be leaving until closing with the hard-on happening under the table.

Nicole clapped her hands smiling, "I knew you'd like it."

Damon would gladly eat the whole damn thing if it meant she would keep smiling at him like that. Damn, he was totally screwed.

They sat finishing off the pizza talking and enjoying each other's company. Just talking, Nicole could really study Damon, like she had never been able to do before. He was so handsome she could almost understand the way women reacted to him. He sat across from her filling his side of the table with broad shoulders, his elbows resting on the table making his biceps bulge just below his short sleeved shirt. Her eyes slowly making their way to his face, she noticed his crooked sexy grin that made her crazy, framing his full mouth.

"Did you hear a word I said?" he leaned back, his golden eyes sparkling with humor.

Crap. No she didn't because she was too busy drooling over his studly body, but she didn't want to let him know that. With the grin he sported, she knew he did anyway. Crap. "Sorry...what?" Smooth Nicole...real smooth.

"I asked you why you haven't taken my head off for giving out our headquarters' number to your clients?" He cocked his eyebrow and damn, didn't that make him even sexier.

Shrugging her shoulders, Nicole wiped her hands on a napkin then tossed it on her plate. "I was going to, but I actually thought about it and figured you're all trained for catching the people responsible. I'm not." At his shocked expression, she laughed. "Yeah, I know my limits, but if the warriors walked away from this problem tomorrow, well, then I'd be back to doing what I was doing before without thought."

"The *without thought* is what scares me," Damon shook his head frowning. "Are you fearless, or do just think you're lucky enough not to end up dead?"

Nicole eyed him for a long minute. "I was afraid for the first eighteen years of my life. I got tired of being afraid of everything and everyone. I have no idea who my parents are. I grew up in the system. I was not one of the lucky ones that was adopted. I went from family to family trying to fit in. The earliest I remember was when I was six. The man and woman who took me in had wanted children, but couldn't. I was there for six months and happy, when she became pregnant. Two weeks later, I was sent back into fostering. The next family I swore to myself would love me. I was seven and the first week I was afraid of them. They acted so nice until my case manager left. I was lucky to eat and when I did, it was what I could find. I was told that if I said anything about what I saw, which was a lot of drugs and drinking, I would be locked in the closet. I was punished a lot and it took me forever to even be able to open a closet door."

Damon sat listening anger simmering his blood, but he didn't say a word feeling her need to let this out.

"They got arrested so I was taken out and put back into the system.

Two more foster families took me in, but it didn't work out for whatever reason. After that, I was in a home for girls until I was sixteen. By then, I didn't want a family, so every time anyone came, I would act up, dye my hair blue or some other ungodly color and they passed me right up. I had only two more years before I was out on my own. Every time people would come, I was afraid to be noticed and wanted. Being wanted and then turned away was worse than anything." Nicole shifted uncomfortably.

"What happened when you were sixteen Nicole?" Damon leaned toward her.

Nicole swallowed visibly. She had never talked about this to anyone and had no idea why she was talking about it now to a guy she had the hots for in a freakin pizza place. Rubbing her hands nervously, she looked away. "It was the last foster family I ever had. It seemed my foster dad had a thing for young girls and my foster mom fed his sickness by doing nothing. It started the second week I was there. He would do and say things that made me uncomfortable. He was good because every time my case manager was there, he found a way to stop us from talking alone." Nicole glanced at him to see his reaction, he just sat listening, his face showing no emotion, but she noticed his eyes were darker than before.

"I knew what was coming and was terrified. Every night for weeks, I would be in bed and hear him stop outside my door, which had no locks plus the doorknob was removed and only put back when the case manager came. I think he was playing mind games. This went on until my seventeenth birthday when I was officially adopted. That night he came to my room and well, tried to do things. I was so afraid and so tired of being afraid. I hid a can of hairspray under my pillow. When he started touching me and stuff, I grabbed the can and sprayed him in the eyes. I ran and never looked back."

Damon had reached over holding her hand rubbing his thumb back and forth on her knuckles. "I'm sorry, Nicole." He would find out who the son of a bitch was and kill him slowly and painfully.

"I didn't tell you this for pity, Damon. I'm telling you this so you

101

understand my mindset." Nicole lifted her chin, "This is why I am the way I am with these kids. I know their fear. I've felt it, tasted it and lived it for the first part of my life. I *will* do everything in my power to keep these kids safe and happy. So when I place one of them in the hands of a monster, I take it very personally. I'm not afraid for me, but I *am* terrified for these kids."

"I don't feel pity for you, Nicole." Damon stared straight into her eyes. "Far from it. I have never met anyone like you before."

Nicole snorted trying to lighten the mood, "I bet you haven't."

Damon smiled then glanced at his watch. "Come on." He stood digging in his pocket to leave a tip. "We need to be at the warehouse in an hour."

Moaning, Nicole stood. "Ugh...can't we call it a night."

Holding the door open for her, he shook his head. "Mitch would have me fired."

Surprised when he took her hand in his, she glanced up at him. He was scanning the parking lot, alert and ready for trouble. Keeping reality in check, she knew his taking her hand was somehow connected to keeping her safe and doing his job, but her heart still skipped a beat at the feel of her hand in his large strong hold.

Damon and Nicole arrived early at the warehouse. They had stopped at her place so she could change, then headed out. Mitch walked in and headed in her direction. Damon was talking to Jared and Duncan while the others, who had dribbled in, started warming up. Nicole had been hitting a heavy bag when Mitch approached.

"How's everything going Callahan?"

"Good." Grabbing her water, she took a swig leaning against the bag she had been warming up on. "Today all my cases went smoothly."

"Any problems other than that?" Mitch eyed her like he was a human lie detector.

"I'm still breathing, so all's good."

"Don't be such a smart ass, Callahan," Mitch growled.

Chuckling, she put her water down, "I'm fine. I think you guys are overreacting about this protection thing, but whatever."

"Yeah well, humor me okay. Until they feel it's safe, you have a round the clock bodyguard."

Nicole rolled her eyes at Mitch who had already turned walking away, and that was when she saw them. Two beautiful women heading toward Damon, Jared and Duncan. The one was the same redhead from before. Glancing down at her old sweats and Snoopy t-shirt, she groaned. God she was pathetic. Turning away, not wanting to see Damon head to the back with any of the women, she started pounding away on the heavy bag.

"PMS or the walking blood banks that just walked in the door?" Pam sneaked up behind her.

"Don't know what you're talking about," Nicole huffed punching the bag with the combination they had been taught to warm up.

"Whatever," Pam chuckled. "Jared told me about the women who are supplied for their *needs*. I mean damn...just look at them. Perfect in every way and their clothes, I mean wow, they must get paid good for this gig cause I couldn't afford the underwear they're probably wearing, if they're even wearing any. I don't see any panty lines under those tight white pants the redhead is wearing like a second skin. Probably a thong. I don't see them wearing granny panties."

"Seriously Pam?" Stopping in mid swing, Nicole turned glaring at Pam sweat sliding down her face. "Why in the hell do you think I care what kind of underwear they're wearing or not wearing?"

Pam gave an innocent shrug, "I was just making innocent conversation. You know, a little gossip."

"There's nothing innocent about you, Pam," Nicole poked a finger at her. "Now let me warm up."

"By all means, beat the holy crap out of the bag," Pam did a sweep of her hand in a courtly manner. "But if I were you, I'd head over there and stake my claim."

"We're just friends," Nicole punched the bag glancing toward Damon who was looking her way at that moment.

"Yeah, with benefits," Pam snorted rolling her eyes. "I call bullshit. Girl, you are halfway in the love with that man, if not already there. You need to go fight for him, because as clear as I can see how you feel about him, I see that redheaded bimbo is ready to stake her claim."

Sighing, Nicole turned once again to Pam and grabbed her shirt thrusting it out. "Look at me Pam. I am no competition for her. I'm wearing a pair of old sweats and a Snoopy t-shirt for shit sake. If *that* is what he wants, then there is nothing I can do."

Pam frowned, "You really don't know how gorgeous you are do you?" Pam really looked wowed. "Even in those ugly ass sweats and t-shirt, you are hands down the most gorgeous woman I have ever known inside and out. I'd do you before I'd do that redhead."

Nicole eyed her funnily, trying to hold in her laughter. "Listen Pam, I love you, I really do, but not that way," Nicole teased

"Bitch," Pam snorted then tackled her to the mat. "Come here and let me lay a wet one on ya."

"What the hell is wrong with you two?" Mitch walked up, hands on his hips, watching the women rolling around laughing and playfully punching each other.

"Pam just proclaimed her secret love for me and I had to turn her down. She didn't take it too well," Laughing, Nicole walked to the center of the mat and plopped down to stretch out.

Damon had seen Nicole's frustration as she beat on the bag and knew the reason. He would feel the same way if another male had been rubbing himself against her, but the bag is not what he would be beating the shit out of. Alice was a beautiful woman, but she was pushy and it was well known she wanted a warrior and wanted one badly. She just wasn't his type and he preferred blondes to redheads, and the blonde he preferred was sitting on the mat looking lost. Pushing himself away from Alice, he headed toward the mat. "You guys go ahead and I'll start class. I'm good."

Jared caught Damon before he made it to the mat. "You need to feed Damon."

"I'm fine, mom." Damon shrugged Jared's hand off his shoulder. "But thanks for worrying."

"If the Council finds out you're not feeding, they 'll pull you and we need you here." Jared glanced toward Nicole, "She needs you here."

"I said I'm fine, Jared." Damon went to walk away and again Jared stepped in his path.

"You cannot and I repeat, *cannot* feed from her," Jared snapped nodding toward Nicole. "If it's Alice, we will call for someone else, but you need to feed and soon dammit."

"I *am* walking away and if you step in my way again, I *will* walk over you," Damon snapped back getting nose to nose with Jared.

"Stubborn son of a bitch." Jared moved to let him pass.

Damon tuned down his anger as he walked to the middle of the mat. He knew the dangers of not feeding and he knew the dangers of feeding from humans, especially humans they were attracted to and he was more than attracted to Nicole. Two things could happen. You either mated with the human which most vampires abhorred, or a blood lust so strong hit that you become a mindless killer. Not only were humans dealing with addiction to their blood, but vampires were fighting addiction to human blood as well. Mitch had been right; it was a cluster fuck of a mess. He should just go grab Alice and feed. It would solve the problem of getting too close to Nicole. No matter what Nicole said, it would hurt her to see him leave with another woman. He would bet his last dollar, he would never be with her again.

With one last look at her, he actually saw relief on her face. God he was screwed because to please her was the only thing that seemed to matter to him. Taking his focus where it belonged, he noticed everyone staring at him waiting for him to start their lessons. "Okay people, let's get a partner and start the defense moves you learned last class," Damon ordered then felt his breath catch when Nicole slipped him a smile. Yep, he was totally screwed.

After their class and shower, Nicole headed over to her bag smiling. It was a good class, but better yet, Damon had not gone into the offices with the redhead and that sent her stomach flipping happily. Damon had gone to shower telling her they would leave as soon as he was done.

"Hey," Pam grabbed her stuff and headed out the door, "I brought that book you wanted to read. I'll grab it and bring it in."

"I'll walk out with you. I have to wait for Damon anyway." Nicole followed Pam outside in the sticky August air.

Pam opened her door grabbing the book. "Don't worry about giving it back. I don't usually reread them." Pam hugged her. "Gotta get. Kenny worked a double, so I want to make sure he has a good dinner tonight."

"Tell him I said hey," Nicole waved watching her friend pull out of the parking lot. Opening the book, she thumbed through it while walking back to the warehouse. A chill shimmied up her spine causing her to look up and then behind her. Suddenly, she didn't feel alone. Flipping the book closed, she turned again to start walking faster and screamed. Standing in front of her was the redhead.

"God, you scared me to death," Nicole laughed nervously bending down to pick up the book she had dropped.

Alice looked her up and down without apology, "Damon needs to feed."

Nicole slowly straightened, instantly on alert, knowing this wasn't going to be a friendly conversation. "And you're telling me this why?"

"I heard Jared and Duncan talking." Alice picked a piece of nonexistent lint off her sleeve. "If Damon doesn't feed soon, they're going to have to tell the Council."

"Damon is a grown man. I'm sure he knows when he has to..." Nicole couldn't bring herself to say feed especially to this women who she knew he had fed from.

"Feed?" Alice gave a nasty laugh. "God, you humans are pathetic. I could kill you with one swipe of my hand. Just hear me out, human. While you may have a little crush on Damon, he will never commit to you. Ever."

"Why are you telling me this?" Nicole was getting angry, but she wasn't stupid enough to go up against this woman since she could actually do what she said. And being killed by Alice with one swipe of her hand, that furnished long sharp red painted nails, was not what she had planned for the evening.

"Because Damon has been good to me. I plan on making him my mate, and nothing will stand in my way. Jared and Duncan agree that you are going to ruin Damon. We've already talked about it and I was elected to fill you in. As long as you're in the picture, Damon is not going to hurt your pitiful little human heart by feeding from me and that will lead to the Council being informed, which in turn will lead to Damon's downfall. He is one of the top warriors and it would be a dishonor for him to be pulled because of blood lust."

"Blood lust?" Nicole hated being ignorant about anything.

"The longer he goes without feeding from one of his own, the more unstable he becomes. Soon, he will lose control and feed from a human, which would probably be you." Alice wrinkled her nose as if the thought disgusted her.

"And that would be bad because...?" God she hated asking this woman these questions, but she needed to know what the hell was going on.

"Oh you poor thing. You really think Damon would want your blood. Look at you." Her laugh was humiliating. "Listen, do yourself a favor and give it up. It's not going to happen. He might be screwing your brains out and believe me I know how good he is at that, but he will never take your blood. He is a warrior and he needs pure vampire blood, my blood."

Okay that hurt, but Nicole hid her emotions because no way would she let this vamp bitch know she was killing her slowly with her words. "Jared and Duncan feel the same way?" She didn't know why she asked it, but the question popped into her head and out of her mouth before she could stop it. She didn't want to think Jared and Duncan had been talking about her and she sure didn't want to be a burden to anyone. No...that place in her life was long gone.

"What, that you're a pathetic human they have to watch over now? Yeah, they do. All they want is for you all to disappear so they can get back to what they were doing before and protect their own kind." Alice smirked, "I cannot believe you can't take a hint. Why humans have been in charge this whole time and we have been in hiding is beyond me. Seriously, if you like Damon at all, leave him alone so he can save face. Jared and Duncan are very concerned and serious about calling the Council." And with that she was gone.

Nicole stood in the parking lot still as stone not knowing what to do. Pain not only about Damon, but the others was too much, overwhelming her with emotions she'd fought so hard her entire life to control. She couldn't face any of them. Seeing Eddie come out of the warehouse, she jogged up to him. "Hey Eddie, can you do me a huge favor?"

Chapter 10

Damon headed out from the back and instantly knew something wasn't right. Looking around, he headed toward Mitch. "Where's Nicole?"

Searching the room, Mitch frowned. "She was just here talking to Pam."

Damon called her name knowing she wouldn't answer. "Son of a bitch." Dropping his stuff, he ran out the door to the parking lot. Nothing. She was nowhere. Rushing back inside, he pulled his phone out. "What's Pam's number?"

Mitch rattled it off pulling his phone out checking to see if he had any messages.

Damon punched in the number pacing back and forth as Jared walked up from the back. "What's going on?" Jared asked Mitch.

"Nicole's gone." Mitch rubbed his eyes trying to stay calm.

Damon snapped his phone shut with a curse, "She said Nicole walked out with her to get a book, and then as Pam was heading inside, she saw Nicole pulling away." Punching in Nicole's number, he prayed she would answer, but knew she wouldn't. Ringing came from the corner; Damon looked over to see her bag laying there. "Shit." He shut his phone and the ringing stopped, a sickening silence followed.

"I'll get Duncan and call Sid. We'll find her." Jared headed toward the back, but stopped when Mitch's phone rang.

"Yeah," Mitch answered. Relief then anger crossed his worried face. "Where the hell are you, Callahan?"

Damon straightened. "Where is she?" He was half way out the door ready to go to her.

Mitch held one finger up to Damon, a finger Damon wanted to break off. His patience was running very thin and he was ready to kill something.

"Nicole don't-" Mitch took the phone from his ear, "hang up. Dammit!"

"Where is she?" Damon demanded still at the door ready to head out after her.

"She's with Eddie." Mitch looked to Jared then back at Damon. "She wanted us to know she was okay, and that she was taking a small leave of absence."

"What the hell brought that on and why did she leave her stuff?" This from Jared. "It doesn't make sense."

"She told me to let her talk and if I interrupted, or anyone else got on the phone, she'd hang up," Mitch frowned.

"That's it?" Damon was pissed, but more than that, he was frantic with worry. She was out there without protection.

"No," he turned to look at Damon. "She told me to tell you, that you needed to feed."

Damon was a blur as he shot across the room grabbing Jared around the throat pinning him to the wall. "You son of a bitch." Damon's deadly hiss cut across the room. "What did you say to her?"

"I didn't say anything Damon." Jared grabbed Damon's arm, but couldn't budge it from his throat. "I would never say anything to hurt that girl and fuck you for thinking I would."

For a second, his hand tightened around his friend's throat before he let go. "Then who did?"

Jared rubbed his throat as understanding flashed in his eyes. "I know who did."

"Alice," both men growled.

***

After thanking Eddie for the ride, she ran into her apartment grabbing things as she went, stuffing them into an overnight bag. She knew Damon would come here first and she had to get out before he showed up. It was cowardly to run off, but she would not be his downfall. Her heart hurt just thinking about it. She would even beg him to go to Alice before she would let him be humiliated before his peers. And with that, she knew Pam was right.

She was in love with him.

Her phone rang in the kitchen spurring her to go faster. Yanking her workout clothes off, she hopped around pulling on a pair of jeans and grabbed a t-shirt throwing it on. The phone went silent for a second before it started to ring again.

Grabbing her bag, she ran to Ren and Stimpy. "Okay guys, watch the place for me." She dribbled food for them. "I'll get Mitch or Pam to feed you until I can get back."

Again, the phone went silent before starting up again driving her crazy; she hated a ringing phone. Taking a quick look around, she grabbed her keys off the counter and headed out the door toward her car. Opening her trunk, she threw in her bag before slamming it shut.

"Going somewhere?" Damon blocked her way to her car door.

Nicole jumped back screaming, tripping over her own feet. Damon reached out to steady her. Gaining control, she pulled away trying to rush past him. "Let me go Damon."

"No." Damon blocked her way again. "Hell, no." He grabbed her keys out of her hand.

"Hey, give those back." Nicole grabbed for them, but he was faster. Sighing, she didn't attempt to take them again. "Damon, please give me my keys."

"Not until you tell me what the hell is going on." Damon leaned up against her car arms crossed, making him seem so at ease. The anger in his eyes told a different story. "Do you know how dangerous it was for you to leave like that without protection?"

"Eddie was with me," Nicole grumbled. Why did he have to look so damn sexy?

Damon rolled his eyes with a snort, "Like I said, without protection." Looking around, he straightened. "As a matter of fact, we should go in. It's not smart standing out in the open like this."

"I don't want to go inside. I want my keys." Nicole was seriously getting pissed. "You are not my boss, father or boyfriend Damon. I am a free woman, able to make my own decisions. Nothing has happened to even hint someone is after me. I want to be left alone and I know you and the others have better things to do than watch after me."

"Who says?" Damon asked, knowing exactly who that was. What he wanted to know is what Alice had said to make her run like that.

"I said," Nicole looked away nervously. She was a horrible liar.

"We *are* going to talk Nicole," Damon glared at her. "Whether you like it or not, whether it's out here or inside, we are going to talk. So I'll give you the option of where you are going to tell me what's going on in that pretty little head of yours."

Nicole felt a warm heat settle in her stomach at the word pretty, then mentally bitch smacked herself. What the hell was wrong with her? She was mad, not all warm and gooey like a teenager with a crush. She was a strong, independent, pissed off woman dammit. "Go to hell." Ha, how about that option vamp, her nose went into the air and she crossed her arms this time.

"That is not an option." Bending over, he tossed her over his shoulder giving her a head rush of deja vu. He carried her inside, fumbled with the keys as he tried to find the right one, when a door behind them opened. Damon turned so fast, Nicole thought she was going to be sick. Seeing an elderly woman peeking out, he relaxed.

"Nicole honey, are you okay?" The woman opened the door wider, her wrinkled face scrunched in concern. "Do you need me to call the police?"

With her butt facing the old woman Nicole pushed off Damon's leg to look around his shapely butt. Seeing the concern on her elderly neighbor's face, made Nicole feel terrible. "No Ms. Webster, I'm fine." Wow, if she kept lying, she might actually get good at it. "He's just helping me inside."

Ms. Webster nodded as if that explained everything when in truth it explained nothing at all, but the old woman just smiled. "Well, you two youngsters have a good night." She winked at Damon who winked back, making the old woman blush to the roots of her white curly hair.

"Lock your door, ma'am," Damon reminded her and didn't turn back around until the click of the lock echoed in the hallway.

Ahhh...how sweet. Nicole got that warm gooey feeling again, then frowned and pinched him on the butt, hard. She kept forgetting she was trying to get rid of him. She squealed when he spanked her hard, then he rubbed it to ease the sting. "Hey, that hurt!"

"So did that pinch, you little hellcat." Damon finally found the right key and shoved the door open slamming it shut with his foot before setting her down.

Blood rushed to her head making her sway. "You really need to stop doing that to me. I think you're giving me brain damage." She watched as he stuck her keys in his pocket and decided to let it go...for now. Glancing at his face, she noticed he had dark circles under his eyes and her heart sunk to her stomach. "You look tired."

Damon ignored her observation, "Why did you run Nicole?"

"Why didn't you feed tonight?" She answered his question with one of her own.

"That's really not your concern." His eyes shifted away from hers.

"It is my concern if I'm being blamed." Nicole sat down heavily on a kitchen stool and sighed, "I won't be your downfall Damon."

Anger blazed across his face. "Listen to me and listen good." Damon stepped toward her leaning down to her face level, "My decision to feed or not feed is my decision."

Nicole jumped up, "Okay, this isn't working." She paced nervously to the kitchen and pulled out a beer wishing it was something stronger. Twisting the cap off, she drank down half the bottle then wiped the back of her hand across her lips. "Maybe I was wrong to leave like I did. I don't want to cause you any problems. I admit that I was just a little jealous of Alice and didn't want to see you around her." She looked away from him, ashamed of herself. She felt like a jealous nag, she hated jealous nags.

"You have no reason to be jealous of her Nicole," Damon shook his head, his sigh echoing in the silence.

God, she was making a mess of this. With one last long swig, she set the beer down. "Listen Damon, I'm going to take a leave of absence from my job. I'll leave town until you all get this under control. I should have done that in the first place."

"Is that really want you want?" Damon asked, his eyes glaring into hers so hard, she knew he was trying to read her.

"Yes," Nicole replied in a strong voice. Yep, she was getting this lying thing down.

"Bullshit," Damon growled. "You love this job, and nothing will stop you from doing it. You said so yourself."

Don't cry she told herself. Do. Not. Cry. "Just please leave, Damon." Nicole couldn't look at him. "Take care of yourself. I'll be fine."

"I'll call Jared and have him come stay with you," he pulled out his phone.

Nicole jumped forward grabbing his hand, "I don't want him here. I don't want any of them here."

What the hell did Alice say to her? If he got his hands on her, he'd wring her no good neck. "Did one of them say something to you?"

"No," she replied quickly. God this was going nowhere. "I just don't want to be a bother to you all anymore."

"You are not a bother to us," Damon touched her cheek and frowned when she jerked away.

"Don't. I can't think when you touch me," Nicole walked backwards running into the stool she'd jumped up from. Reaching behind her, she steadied the stool wishing she could steady herself as easily.

A sexy grin curved his lips for a slight second, pleased that his touch affected her as much as her touch sent him reeling. He wanted to kiss that unhappy frown from her lips, but knew he had to take care of this situation because if he didn't, she'd run again. "I know Alice talked to you." Seeing the surprise flash across her face, told him that he and Jared had been right on. "I want to know what she said to you."

"I don't know what you're talking about," Nicole glanced down staring at her feet. She didn't want to relive that conversation and she was embarrassed to think that Jared and Duncan thought she was a burden and hurting Damon.. Her feet started to blur as tears filled her eyes. Do. Not. Cry. She repeated the words she grew up repeating over and over again. Her head flew up when she heard Damon on the phone.

"Did you find her?" he asked into the phone. "Okay. Pick her up. We're on our way."

"What are you doing?" Nicole eyed the phone. "Who was that?"

"Get your stuff." Damon walked toward her. "If you aren't going to tell me what happened, then I'll find out myself."

"No," Nicole whispered in horror. "No!"

"Then tell me, because one way or another, I am going to find out." Damon shoved his phone in his back pocket and pulled her keys out of his front pocket.

Nicole's face burned. He was backing her in a corner and she didn't like it. "Why are you doing this?" Nicole felt her anger hitting a dangerous level. "Just leave it alone."

"I don't like anyone hurting you." Damon crossed the room causing her to back up a step, "I won't tolerate it. I know Alice and how she is."

Okay, she didn't expect that. Never in her whole life had anyone showed this much protection toward her and she didn't know how to handle it. She searched his golden eyes, his expression, and realized that he really meant what he said. Feeling tears leaking out the corner of her eyes, she quickly turned away panicked. She would not cry in front of him. She cried in front of no one. Hell, she hardly ever cried at all. It showed weakness. She had learned not to do that at a very young age.

"Nicole?" Damon walked up behind her touching her gently on the shoulder.

"Oh, God." His closeness, his touch, his voice was all it took to break her. Great heavy sobs overtook her body. She doubled over, arms crossed over her stomach. Years of tears burst free dripping to the floor. It was all too much. Harsh reality squeezed her heart in a painful grip.

Damon grabbed her, picking her up with care, carrying her to the couch. "Let it out," Damon whispered, his lips pressed to her head that was cradled against his chest. Her pain tore at him, a pain more intense than anything he'd ever experienced before. He didn't say anything else. There was nothing to say. He just held her as she let all the pain and craziness of her life out in a good old fashion cry.

"I got your shirt all wet," Nicole sniffed wiping at her eyes feeling like a total idiot. "I'm sorry. I never cry," she looked away embarrassed.

Damon lifted her chin with a finger, looking into her eyes. "You can get my shirt wet anytime you need to." He brushed a stray tear escaping down her flushed cheek. "I bet you haven't had a good cry in quite some time."

"I haven't cried since I was really little," Nicole answered honestly. "Shows weakness, and in my case, weakness was not a trait I could afford to have."

"I'm sorry you had to live that way." Damon cradled her head back to his chest. "But it's made you the woman you are today. A woman I respect deeply."

Okay, that sent the warm sensations swarming through her body. "Thank you. That means a lot to me," Nicole whispered, touched. Then her head popped up panicked. "Please call whoever you called and tell them not to bring Alice anywhere to meet us."

"First, you tell me what happened." Damon wasn't going to budge. "I don't leave things undone. I want to hear from you what happened."

With a deep stuttering breath, Nicole told him about her conversation with Alice and actually felt a little better.

Holding his anger in check was the hardest thing he had ever done, but he didn't want Nicole to think it was directed at her. "Alice has tried for years to be mated to me," Damon explained. "She obviously feels threatened by you and decided to scare you off, and it almost

118

worked. I have never been with her other than feeding-"

"Damon, you don't have to explain this to me. It's really none of my business who you're with or have been with," Nicole broke in pushing herself off his lap, but he held her not letting her go.

"I know I don't, but I want to." Damon grasped her chin gently bringing her face up to meet his, brushing his thumb back and forth across her tear stained cheek. "I have only fed from her Nicole. The same with Jared and Duncan. We pick who we have relationships with, not the Council."

She saw in his eyes the truth and felt totally stupid for acting like a jealous idiot. This was all new to her. She avoided relationships because of this very thing. She didn't want to...hurt and the worst hurt is loving and not being loved back. "I'm sorry Damon," Nicole sniffed reaching up touching his hand that held her chin. "I just don't want to be a problem to anyone. I can't change that about myself."

"I don't want you to change, but I do want you to trust me to know what is good for you to stay safe." Damon brought his other hand up and cupped her face, "Just trust me, Nicole."

Nodding, Nicole's stomach flipped and flopped in anticipation. Never had she had a man hold her as delicately or stare so intently into her eyes. Licking her bottom lip, she watched his eyes change from concern to blazing desire. His head dipped and he ran his tongue along the same path hers had just taken. With a moan, she touched her tongue to his. One hand slid to the back of her head, grabbing her hair, tilting her head back before plunging deeply into her mouth. His other hand went to the small of her lower back pushing her tightly against him. Straddling him, she could feel his cock swell against her; she wanted nothing more in the world than for him to take her hard right then, right there. To hell with everything. The only thing that mattered to her at the moment was Damon.

It took both of them a minute to hear someone pounding on the door. Damon pulled away so quickly, she would have fallen backward off his lap if he hadn't caught her. Picking her up, he stood and hurriedly set her down in front of her room, gently pushing her inside. "Stay there and keep this door shut," he ordered closing the door. Damon the lover was gone, replaced by Damon the protector.

Heart pounding, Nicole quietly cracked her door open to peek out in time to see Jared come through the door. Closing the door with a click, her stomach clinched. She didn't want to see Jared yet. She was just processing her issues with Damon. Walking to her bed, she crawled to the middle cuddling a pillow to her stomach. Minutes passed before her door opened.

Damon instantly found Nicole huddled on her bed looking pale. "It's just Jared, but I guess you knew that since you disobeyed me by opening your door."

She started to argue, but stopped with a sigh, "I just wanted to make sure you were okay." She shrugged. "What does he want?"

Damon crossed the room towering over her, touched by her concern for him. "He brought your phone and bag you left at the gym." He handed it to her. "I need to take care of something, so he's going to stay here until I can get back."

Anxious, Nicole sat up on her knees. "I'll be fine Damon. He doesn't need to stay." At his frown, she sat back down. "Never mind. Tell him thanks."

"Why don't you tell him?" Damon pushed, wanting to get this crap Alice started behind them.

"I'm pretty tired," she lied laying back then curling up on her side. "Think I'll hit the hay. Will you be back tonight?"

"He wants to talk to you." Damon grabbed her hand and pulled her up, "Come on."

Nicole sighed following him out of her bedroom. She expected him to drop her hand as soon as they went out to her small living room, but he held it tighter. Glancing from the floor to Jared, she was shocked when he walked over and hugged her tightly.

"You scared the shit out of us Nicole." Jared pulled back glaring at her. "Don't ever do that again."

At first, Nicole couldn't find her voice. To say she was shocked was an understatement. "I'm sorry I didn't mean to cause a problem."

Anger flushed his face. "I know what Alice said to you, and it was all bullshit."

Totally uncomfortable with the situation, Nicole backed away attempting to let go of Damon's hand, but he wasn't having any of it. His grip tightened and he pulled her closer to him. "Listen, I really just want to forget about the whole thing," Nicole tried to smile, but hurt still bubbled to the surface. "I shouldn't have left like I did, and I won't again."

"Did you hear what I said?" Jared eyed her knowing she had, but it didn't penetrate. "Alice is trying to cause trouble and it isn't going to work. As warriors, we have taken an oath to protect and like it or not, you're under our protection. It's what we do and honey. I have to say, you've been the most entertaining person I've ever had the pleasure of protecting."

Smiling sadly, Nicole walked up to him and kissed him lightly on the cheek. "Thank you."

Jared again pulled her into a hug, "Anytime honey."

"Kiss her and I'll break your face," Damon frowned pulling Nicole out of his friends embrace and into his.

Jared grinned and winked at her, "Jealous much bro?"

Damon ignored him as Nicole tilted her face up to his. "I'll be back as soon as I can." Leaning down, he brushed a kiss across her lips. He looked at Jared, all tenderness gone from his face. "Take care of her."

121

Then he was gone.

Jared rubbed his hands together, "Okay Nicole, what kind of trouble can we get into?"

Feeling better, Nicole laughed. "You play Call of Duty?"

"The question human is, do you?" Jared headed toward the PlayStation. "Cause I'm no gentleman when it comes to Call of Duty, so prepare to get your ass shot off."

"In your dreams vamp," Nicole teased. "And since when have you ever been a gentleman."

Jared turned to give her a glare, then grinned. "You got a point there."

Shaking her head, she grabbed two beers from the fridge and hunkered down for a night of gaming.

Chapter 11

Chad stood in the middle of a small, dark and nasty smelling room wondering for the hundredth time if he had truly lost his mind. Memories of the night at the hospital haunted him. No, he hadn't lost his mind, revenge had overtaken it. The need for revenge was strong filling his every second, making him sick with hate.

"You got the money?" A raspy voice echoed from a dark corner of the room.

Chad tossed the envelope on the table next to him, "It's all there. Count it if you want."

Long pale fingers reached out from the darkness tapping the envelope with one long pointed fingernail. "You sure about this human? Usually it is you bringing me treats to feed my hunger. Their blood is so sweet and tangy."

No, he wasn't fucking sure about this, Chad thought, but straightened up. Too much depended on this transaction, and he'd be damned if he backed out now. He had some paybacks to dish out, and this was his only option. "Yeah, I'm sure, so let's do this before I change my mind." The envelope disappeared into the darkness.

"There's no going back," the voice deepened as it appeared out of the darkness.

"No shit," Chad watched the body behind the voice come into the shadowy light, and knew he was totally screwed. Red eyes glowed from the darkness as the figure moved toward him. God this was crazy, but if he didn't take care of that bitch and her bloodsucking hero, he was as good as dead anyway. This was the only way. Not a praying man, he sent one up anyway hoping the big guy would hear his one last request to survive what was to come.

"Any last requests human?"

"Yeah, make it quick." Chad stepped back, his eyes growing wide as he got the first look at the horrendous image behind the voice. "Oh, God."

"Don't think God's gonna help you now," the evil laugh echoed through the dark room.

Chad screamed as he was attacked. His last thought was of the bitch and her lover dying by his hand. Soon, very soon.

The screams stopped, the only sound in the dark room was the sloppy grotesque sounds of Chad's blood being sucked from his body.

***

Nicole was the next player up to bat. The charity softball game looked to be a hit, no pun intended, and she loved it. All proceeds went to the shelters in the county to help with the crazy costs involved.

It had been two days since Damon had left her in Jared's care in which she beat Jared in their war on Call of Duty. She didn't ask where Damon had been or why, but she would trust him to feed like he was supposed to; he looked better since that night, so she knew he had fed, but what she was totally confident about was that it wasn't from Alice.

She had tried to get Damon, Jared and Duncan to play in the softball game, but they refused insisting they would be there to support. She'd huffed, and finally left them alone mumbling chicken shits under her breath a few times.

"Get your head out of your butt Callahan, you're up," Mitch yelled from third base where he wore the coach's shirt proudly, and most definitely a little too seriously. It was, after all, a fun charity game. Yeah, right. In Mitch's eyes, this was the World Series of all World Series. She had warned Mitch and the others that all curse words would be a dollar if caught since so many kids attended the game. It was kind of funny to watch Mitch's frustration at not being able to say what he wanted. Catching Damon's eye in the stands, she smiled when he winked. Jared stood whooping and whistling for her. God, how embarrassing. She shook her head with a grin.

Sid had volunteered to ump for them since no one would argue too much with the badass vamp. These games, even for charity, got a little heated. They, the Cincy Cyclones, were going against the Newtown Tigers. Rivals for years at these charities, but all in good fun.

Nicole took her place and readied herself to bat more nervous than ever because she could feel Damon's eyes on her. What that man could do to her with just his eyes alone was unnerving. She glanced over at Mitch who was doing all kinds of weird stuff with his hands and hat. She had no clue, and neither did he, equally oblivious to the signs meant, but he said it would throw off the other team...yeah, right.

"Strike," Sid yelled as the ball came sailing by her.

Okay, now that looked like a ball to her. Eying Sid for a second, she then focused on the pitcher.

"Got a problem with that call?" Sid asked from behind his ump mask.

"Would it matter if I did?" she countered.

"Nope," he chuckled liking his power position.

"You need me to slow that down a little bit Callahan?" Jim Blevins, the other team's pitcher snorted loudly.

"Give me what you got Blevins," Nicole called back. She had played high school and college softball along with summer leagues, so he had nothing on the girls who'd pitched to her before. Far from it. This time, she made contact dropping the ball behind second base. Making it to first, she glanced at Mitch who stood at his coaching spot with his arms spread wide.

"Lay off the candy Callahan and you probably could have made it to second," Mitch hollered before focusing on Pam who was up. Immediately, he started his signs again.

Pam kept jumping out of the batter's box afraid of getting hit, but earned a walk. Pam pranced her way to first as Nicole headed to second. Next up was Eddie who hit to center field sending Nicole running and rounding third with Mitch whipping his arms around for her to go home. Seeing the catcher stooping, she knew the ball was coming so she slid feet first just as the catcher got the ball.

"Out!" Sid who had thrown his mask off yelled. Boo's and yells were shouted from the stands. Mitch was storming to home plate yelling.

"Would hate to be you right now," Nicole chuckled knowing his call was right on. She was out and that's why she wasn't in his face right now, vampire or not.

"Get back to your base coach," Sid pointed at Mitch who was pointing his hat at Sid yelling. "Go, before I throw you out." Sid wasn't taking any of Mitch's crap.

After their three outs, Mitch was giving them their positions, leaving Nicole for last. "Callahan, go to center field."

"No," Damon, who came up behind her, answered before she could head out. "I can't protect her out there."

"Damon, I'll be fine," Nicole sighed. "No one is going to do anything with this many people around."

Damon eyed Mitch, not budging. "First base," Mitch nodded.

"I don't play bases," Nicole refused not wanting to sound like a baby, but wanting to play where she knew she could do well. She hated playing bases and sucked at it.

"For shit sake," Mitch grumbled. "Take short stop and send Eddie to center."

Both Nicole and Mitch looked at Damon who was staring at where short stop would be. When he nodded, Nicole grabbed her glove and headed out on the field. Damon headed around the dugout toward short stop where he would be close. Jared was close behind him.

Damon stood on the sidelines, his senses on full alert. He knew it was a matter of time before a hit was made. The longer it took, the more alert he became because he knew it was coming. These people didn't give up until they got what they wanted and they wanted Nicole dead. Exactly who wanted her dead, was still a mystery.

After getting the lay of everything, Damon relaxed enough to watch the game. He was surprised at how good a player Nicole actually was. He really shouldn't be surprised. He watched as she played her position good heartedly taunting the other team and laughing when they taunted back at her. Her blonde hair was pulled up in a sloppy ponytail, her ball cap pulled low over her eyes. She was one of the shortest players on the field, but she played with no fear diving for balls, throwing people out, all the while being the most beautiful woman, inside and out, he had ever known. The thought of someone wanting to hurt her sent anger surging through his body.

Cheering the last out, Nicole started to head to their dugout as she looked over at Damon and stopped, her hands still together in a clap. It was as if her whole body stopped except for her heart which beat a hard frantic tempo in her chest. His stare was so intense it made her shiver and her legs feel like rubber. Her feet started toward him until Pam slapped her arm around her shoulders leading her toward the dugout talking a mile a minute. Peeking over Pam's shoulder, Damon walked along slightly behind them outside of the field, but his eyes never left her. "Wow..." Nicole whispered looking away, her body having all kind of needy feelings running rampant.

"Wow what?" Pam chuckled looking closely at Nicole. "Why are you so flushed? You getting too hot?"

"Yeah, too hot," Nicole giggled shaking her head. Damn that vamp was going to cause her to have a freakin heat stroke.

The game continued, but Nicole was too busy watching Damon. He hadn't looked at her much since and she willed him to do again. The feeling was outrageous. She knew she wasn't one of those women who needed a man to make her life better, but man, it had felt good and she would like to have that feeling just one more time...dammit.

"Strike!" Sid yelled from behind home plate.

Nicole glared back at him. Crap, she was batting and staring at Damon. What the hell was she doing?

"What?" Sid flipped his mask up glaring back at her. "You want a do over?"

"What in blue blazes are you waiting for Callahan?" Mitch yelled in his annoying coach voice. "Hit the little white ball."

Glaring at the catcher when he chuckled, she got in her ready stance and concentrated on the pitcher. She swung and missed.

"Strike two!" Sid yelled.

"How'd ya like that one Callahan? If you need a more girlie throw, I can do that for ya." He demonstrated by taking a slow step forward like he was going to toss it nice and slow underhand.

"Crap," Nicole hissed under her breath. A-hole out there was not going to strike her out. "Come on, stop taunting like a girl and throw the ball," Nicole grinned as Jim's face flushed in anger. Nicole watched the ball all the way in and swung as hard as she could. The bat and ball connected almost taking Blevins' head off. Dropping the bat, she took off to first then rounded to go to second, but stopped when she saw Blevins screaming and yelling, heading right for her.

"You did that on purpose," Jim bellowed as the benches cleared, players yelling over each other.

"Jim, you know that's not true," Nicole chuckled backing away

128

knowing that Jim was just kidding. "Cause if I would have done that on purpose, I would have hit ya." Nicole glanced over to see Jared holding Damon back. She gave him a thumbs up letting him know she was okay. They always ended the games with a bench clearing so both teams got thrown out and no one was really a winner. It was after all a charity event, not a regular season game which she played on through the summer.

Soon everyone was laughing walking off the field while the spectators cheered and headed toward the food. Nicole had lost sight of Damon, but saw Jared waiting for her.

"Nice game," he grinned. "Thought you were going to behead the big guy for a minute."

Nicole chuckled shaking her head. "Nah, Blevins isn't a bad guy. Just talks a lot of smack and I wanted to take him down a peg or two, not kill him."

"He went to cool down," Jared answered the question she hadn't asked, but wanted to badly. "Thought he was going to kill that guy when he charged you yelling."

"Sorry, I should have warned you guys about the way we end the games. It was a big hit the first time it happened for real when the benches cleared, so we all decided to end them all that way having both teams thrown out so no winners." Nicole waved to a couple of people who walked by. Then she spotted him standing alone. Without saying anything, she headed toward him.

"What are you doing over here?" Nicole smiled adjusting her heavy ball bag up on her shoulder.

Without saying a word, Damon lifted the bag off her shoulder and slung it up on his. "How much longer?"

"It's going to be a while yet." Nicole glanced behind her watching the hungry mob attack the food tables. "You hungry? I'm starving."

Damon glanced at the crowd with a frown. "Not really."

Feeling disappointed, Nicole sighed. "I can't leave Damon, but if you want to then I'm sure Jared and Sid will stay.

Shaking his head, he nudged her toward the crowd. "Come on," Damon grumbled. "Just don't blame me if I accidentally kill that pitcher."

Nicole laughed with a cock of her shaped eyebrow. "Accidentally?" Shaking her head at his serious expression, she laughed again. "Jim wasn't going to hurt me, Damon. I could probably take him with all those fancy moves you've taught me. It was all a show for the crowd and to end the game on an even keel."

This time Damon's eyebrow cocked up into his runaway bangs. "Fancy moves?" Damon frowned. "I teach sensible killing moves to keep you alive, not fancy."

Rolling her eyes, Nicole chuckled grabbing his arm. "Come on before all the food is gone. I'm starving."

"For as little as you are, you sure do eat a lot," Damon teased.

"You ain't seen nothing yet buddy." Nicole liked this teasing banter they had going on.

Damon smiled down at her before following her toward the food. The rest of the night was spent talking and eating. Nicole was happy to see that Duncan had brought Steve, who was now talking to a girl his age and seemed to be charming her. Yeah, she knew how the poor girl felt. Damon was doing the same thing to her. He was polite to everyone, even Jim who he talked motorcycles talk with.

Nicole heard her phone ringing in her baseball bag and dug for it. Glancing at the number she didn't recognize, she flipped it open. "Hello." When no one replied she pressed her palm against her free ear cutting out most of the noise around her and walked a few steps away "Hello."

"So you think you're safe?" The deep voice on the other end hissed.

"Who is this?" Nicole replied, a wicked chill skimming up her spine as she took a step toward Damon

"Do not take another step," the voice demanded. "Before I kill you, I've decided to make you suffer."

Oh God, he was here somewhere. Damon was still talking, but had turned his body toward her instead of her being at his back. Everything seemed to be moving in slow motion. "Who is this?" she whispered knowing she wouldn't get an answer, but she did and it was one she would never forget.

"Your worst nightmare," he rasped with a chuckle. "I'll give you five seconds to save your boss."

Nicole gasped looking desperately for Mitch. "What?" her voice shook not understanding until she saw the red dot on Mitch's forehead. "Oh God, no!"

"One," the man counted out.

With no thought to anything but Mitch, Nicole took off running, knocking people out of her way. She heard Damon yelling for her as heavy footsteps pounded behind her. Reaching Mitch, she heard the sound a gun shot just as she jumped at Mitch, tackling him to the ground. The wooden fence splintering where his head had been. Screams and panic sent people running. A heavy weight landed on top of Nicole.

"Are you hit?" Damon ran his hands frantically over her body checking. "Goddammit Nicole, are you hit?"

It took her a minute to get her bearings. "No," Nicole shook her head. "I'm fine. Are you okay Mitch?"

"I'm fine." Shaken, Mitch looked up at the fence which had a huge

Damon watched her closely. He knew she was on the edge and was just waiting for her to plunge over. A lesser woman would have collapsed under the shit Nicole had been thrust into over the past week. Week, hell, just today. First Mitch, and now this.

Dread so strong burned in her chest as she looked over to where Ren and Stimpy made their home. Nicole cried out, "Nooooo." She ran to the shattered bowl searching for her turtles. People had dogs, cats, birds, but Nicole had her turtles that she loved. Seeing Ren on his back laying still under the table their rocky home sat on, she knelt down ignoring the broken glass digging into her hands and knees. Carefully picking him up, she prayed he was okay. Turning him over, bile pushed to the back of her throat at the words crudely carved into his shell - SUFFER. "Ren, come on...come out." She taped on the shell which both turtles responded to, but this time instead of his head poking out the turtles long neck flopped forward, the head gone.

Hearing the keening noise coming from Nicole's throat, Damon reached down and pulled her up taking the turtle from her. When he caught this fucking guy, he was going to show the bastard what suffering meant. Pulling her into his arms, he pressed her head into his chest and reached for his phone. "Jared get over to Nicole's fast, bring Sid and Patrick." He clicked the phone closed seeing the other turtle laying a few feet away with the word BITCH carved into its shell. Yeah, the bastard was gonna pay.

Chapter 12

Nicole kept busy in the days that followed the break in at her apartment. Slowly, her apartment had taken shape to where it looked almost as it had before, with no hint of a break in, except for the small table Ren and Stimpy had called home for years. It stood empty, a gruesome reminder of what had happened. A knock on her office door sent the unhappy memories to the back of her mind. "Come in."

Pam stuck her head in the door, her face showing signs of strain. "Mitch wants you in his office pronto and boss-zilla is in there with him."

"Great," Nicole tossed the file she had been updating. Joining Pam in the hall, she really took a closer look at her friend. "You okay? Sorry, but you look like crap."

Pam's eyes shifted before turning back to Nicole. "Yeah, just stuff at home. No biggie."

Feeling like the worst friend in the world, Nicole sighed. "I'm sorry, Pam. I've been so caught up in my own drama that I-"

"Hey, don't sweat it," Pam stopped her. "It's not a big deal. Just tired and cranky. PMS and all that jazz. Now go on before boss-zilla comes a huntin."

Nicole watched as her friend headed down the hall, her step not as light as it usually was. Making a mental note to pick up on this conversation after her office visit with Mitch, she turned and headed toward his office hearing his voice booming from behind his closed door. "Ugh....don't want to go in there," Nicole sighed to the empty hallway. Damon had left on an errand, but Jared was in one of the offices looking through case files to find any clue that might lead them to the master mind behind the blood trafficking. They had added so much security stuff to the building, she doubted the US Army could breech the doors.

Closing her eyes briefly, she sucked it up and knocked before opening the door. "You wanted to see me boss?"

"Yes, we did," Catherine Ross, aka boss-zilla, replied from behind Mitch's desk tapping the end of a pencil on a stack of files. "Sit down Ms. Callahan."

Nicole glanced at Mitch who wouldn't meet her stare. He leaned against the far wall staring a hole in the side of Catherine's brown bobbed head. Taking a seat where she could look at them both, she remained silent, her sixth sense telling her that she was not going to like what happened in the next second. Looking at Catherine, who had no problem looking her in the eyes, Nicole thought she'd be pretty if wasn't for the permanent scowl on her face. She was a short woman, but she packed so much attitude, she seemed as tall as Mitch, even though her feet probably didn't touch the floor as she sat in Mitch's chair.

"I am just going to come to the point," Catherine began, the tapping of the pencil stopped. "You are being placed on a mandatory leave of absence as of this minute. We will hold your job until the danger to you is over."

"But..." Nicole leaned out of her seat ready to do battle.

"I said mandatory, Ms. Callahan," Catherine's voice was level and sure. "There are no negotiations in this matter. Not only are you in danger, but as the incident the other night at the charity game proved, others are in danger also."

Nicole quickly glanced at Mitch who finally glanced her way. "I'm sorry Nicole, there's nothing I can do."

"He's right. This is happening and if I feel that there is too much resistance in this matter, I have the authority to terminate, which includes, anyone who tries to interfere." She eyed Mitch with a cock of her nicely shaped brow.

"But they're after me." Nicole knew she was fighting a losing battle, but dammit she had to try. This was her job, her life.

For a minute, it looked like Catherine's eyes filled with sympathy, but then the boss-zilla side overcame and the scowl quickly replaced it. "What happened at the charity game was because of you Nicole. We cannot take the chance of another employee getting in the line of fire or one of the children in your care."

Nicole hadn't thought of that or maybe she had and was just too selfish to see it that way. Confusion and a sense of loss hit her, feelings of defeat came at her in waves. "I don't want that to happen. I guess you're right." God those words tasted bitter.

"Listen, as soon as this blows over and they catch whoever this is, your job will be waiting for you." Catherine stood picking up her briefcase, "I'm sorry it has come to this Nicole, but it's not worth the risk."

"I understand," Nicole nodded, waiting for her to leave.

Boss-zilla had a few words with Mitch before he closed the door to his office and sat heavily at his desk looking haggard. "Dammit!" he hissed, not looking at her.

"She's right, Mitch." Nicole looked up smiling sadly. "In all my standing up for my job, I really didn't think what the consequences could be for others. I could never live with myself if something happened to someone here at work, or God forbid, one of the kids. Just so much is happening so quickly I haven't thought it through. I'll just get my stuff and leave."

Mitch stood with her, "Keep yourself safe until this bastard is caught. I need you here. The kids need you here."

Nodding, Nicole stopped before walking out the door. "Who's taking my cases?"

Mitch stared at her for a long moment, "I am, so don't worry about anything. I'll keep you informed on all of them."

Turning quickly, she gave him a tight hug, and then without meeting his gaze, she hurried out of his office before she could breakdown. "Thanks Mitch," she called out. "And don't mess up my filing system," she added the teasing remark despite the tears that filled her eyes.

Once in her office, Nicole stuffed as much as she could in a backpack she had in her office, then left making her way to where Jared was. She better let someone know where she was going. She made enough mistakes by taking off and didn't want to cause more of a stir than she already had. Walking into the office where Jared sat at a table with files laying all around him, she cleared her throat. "Find anything yet?"

Jared glanced up rubbing the bridge of his nose. "Maybe," he sighed. "Have you noticed that a lot of Chad's cases were older boys?"

Sitting down across from him, she dropped her backpack. "No, not really," Nicole frowned. "Why would that make a difference? I mean most of the cases we get are predetermined by someone else. Most of the time Mitch."

"I understand that, but most of them have an addendum stating that he requested the older boys ages 13 to 17."

"What difference does that make?" Nicole's troubles were soon forgotten as her interest piqued.

"Because, the blood of a vampire becomes more potent the older the vampire gets." Jared leaned back in his chair. "Have you ever tried Crimson Rush before?"

Nicole looked horrified, "God, no!"

Jared chuckled, "I bet you'd drink Damon's."

"And you'd lose that bet," she snorted.

"He hasn't taken yours either?" he squinted at her.

"No." Embarrassed, she glanced away. Being with a vampire that didn't yearn for your blood was pretty much a confidence killer. God, how screwed up was she to want someone to want her blood. Ugh...she was truly losing it.

"Do you know that if you were to mate with a vampire, it's for life and you would need their blood?" Jared watched her closely, a secret smile playing across his lips.

"I heard something like that, but that's just with vampires." Nicole replied. She wanted to ask more, but didn't want to look too pathetic by wanting to know more about human and vampire relationships. "I mean a vampire and human can't be mated."

"Nope," Jared tried not to chuckle. He loved messing with this woman.

"Nope what?" Nicole frowned. "Nope I'm right they can't, or nope I'm wrong they can?"

"I can see right through you Nicole," Jared laughed shaking his head. "Nope you're wrong. We can mate with humans. It totally depends on our responses. Some call it magic if you believe in that sort of thing."

"Well, I didn't believe in you guys, so magic doesn't seem so far fetched now does it," Nicole grinned.

"I don't know what it is really and I've lived this life for hundreds of years. I do know when you find your mate, it is like nothing you've ever felt. If we mate with a human, our blood is their substance to keep them young and alive. If a human's vampire mate dies, the human dies, unless she takes to another vampire."

"Why not just turn the human?" Nicole wondered aloud.

"Not all humans live through the change, so most vampires don't chance losing their mates." Jared leaned back to the table shuffling through files.

"Have you ever found a mate?" Nicole asked curious.

Jared stopped in mid shuffle, his eyes flashing straight to hers. "No, I haven't," Jared replied. "Hopefully, before my time ends, I will have found that perfect someone. I've seen it with others and it's intense once they're mated. It's a love that nothing or no one can ever come between."

Nicole sat in thought wondering what that would feel like to be loved like that by another person, vampire or human. She had never felt love in any fashion or form, but she knew her feelings were strong for a certain vampire and that scared the crap out of her. What if Damon found his mate? How would she cope with that? Feeling her stomach clench at the thought, Nicole stood up wanting to change the subject. "Do you think you could take a break and take me home?" Nicole hated being a burden in any sense.

"What, you playin' hooky the rest of the day?" Jared joked, but seeing her face, he turned serious.

"What is it Nicole?" Jared stood, walking toward her.

"I've been placed on a mandatory leave of absence. It seems I'm too dangerous to have around." Nicole shrugged her shoulder hating the fact she was starting to feel sorry for herself and damn, didn't that rub her the wrong way.

"Ahhh...I'm sorry." Jared placed a large hand on her shoulder. "Things just aren't going your way are they?"

A bitter laugh escaped her lips, "As Mitch would say, my life has turned into a real shit storm." Nicole grabbed her bag.

Damon pulled up on his bike as they were heading to Jared's car. "What's wrong?" Damon demanded watching Nicole closely. "I told you I would be back for you."

"I've been put on mandatory leave of absence," Nicole frowned, hating repeating the news over again.

Nodding, Damon didn't question it, which she fell a little more in love with him for. She really didn't want to talk about it. "Come on," Damon replied making room on the bike. She swung her backpack on her back and climbed on.

Jared smiled with a wink at Nicole. Grabbing the helmet tied to the back of Damon's bike, Jared placed it on her head, buckled it under her chin then tapped the top of it. "Cargo is ready to go," Jared chuckled at Nicole's scowl.

Nicole wrapped her arms around Damon's waist pressing her face against his strong back. God, she loved the bike. She felt so free every time they rode it, like flying. Every time she asked him to go faster, he would refuse saying he wouldn't risk getting her hurt which was sweet, but aggravating.

Taking the old road next to the river, Nicole watched the passing scenery trying to forget the last forty-eight hours of her messed up life. Wrapping her arms tighter around Damon's waist, she decided to ask one more time. "Please go faster Damon," she called out over the roar of the wind.

This time Damon shifted and they were flying down the road, the scenery, passing so fast, she couldn't make it out anymore. Smiling, she let everything go at that moment except for the feeling of the bike under her and the vampire in front of her.

Chapter 13

Damon opened the door to her apartment and did the 'all clear' thing, as usual making her wait just inside the door. She dropped her backpack on the floor and waited to get that homey feeling she always got when coming home to her tiny apartment, but it didn't come. She was afraid it never would. Damon flashed back to her side in a second after checking every corner of her place.

"It's safe," Damon glanced down at her intently.

Nicole nodded walking further into her apartment glancing to the table, which had been empty since the break-in, out of habit. This time something was sitting on it. Curious, Nicole took a few steps and stopped, her hand flying to her mouth. Walking quickly to the large bowl, she looked down seeing two turtles lazily laying on rocks sunning under the lamp Damon had placed over them. Tears filled her eyes blurring the small turtles.

"I know it's not Ren and Stimpy, but..."

Nicole threw herself at him not letting him finish, practically crawling up his body holding on tight, her face buried in his neck breathing in his scent.

He chuckled, "Ah...you're welcome?" He held her just as tight before gripping her hair gently in his fist pulling her head back to look into her intense watery eyes.

"No one has ever done anything like that for me before," her voice was raspy with emotion, cracking at the end. "Thank you so much." Since her legs were wrapped around his waist, his arm tucked around her holding her to him, she took both of her hands and cupped his face lightly, kissing his full lips.

Damon would get her a fucking zoo full of animals if this was how she thanked him, but his protective instincts hit full force and he eased away from her kiss and damn, wasn't that the hardest thing he'd ever done. Once with her was no way enough, but it was too dangerous right now to lose himself in the sweet body so temptingly wrapped around his. Slowly, he eased her down his body. "What are you going to name them?"

Embarrassed heat colored her cheeks as he set her away from him. "Sorry, I didn't mean to jump you." She turned away, "Just wanted to thank you."

Damon grabbed her before she could move away, "Honey, you can thank me any time." He leaned down kissing her lightly on the lips. "But my main concern right now is keeping you alive, and having you wrapped around me like that...well, let's just say, protecting isn't what I want to be doing to you," he flashed her some fang with the sexy grin he tossed her way.

Nodding with a smile, Nicole glanced again at the turtles and knew without a doubt, she had fallen in love with this man. "You hungry?"

His eyes roamed down her body slowly then back up, his eyes darker than before. "Starved."

Her hand rubbed her stomach while it did that funny floppy feeling it always did around Damon. "We have locks on the door you know." Nicole walked over sliding the dead bolt with a loud click. "And didn't Sid put a sensor thingy around the windows and stuff?"

Damon's lips curved as he nodded slowly, watching her under lowered lashes.

"I've had a really hard day with having to leave my job, and I really need a friend right now. Don't you have special senses like Spider-man's spidey senses to know if the bad guys are coming?" Nicole was having fun watching Damon's eyes turn dark and hot as he watched her. God, to have a little power over a man like this was mind blowing. "That's kind of a turn-on you know. He could probably do all kinds of things to Mary Jane and still know if the bad guys were coming so he could protect her."

"Spiderman's a pussy," Damon growled, pinning her to the wall. His body caging her in, his head bowed next to her ear. "You're playing with fire human."

"I like fire vamp," Nicole's husky reply brushed across his chest.

Tipping her face up with his finger under her chin, he smiled down at her. "As much as I would love to take you against this wall, I'm not going to." His smile grew and he chuckled at her moan. "Listen and listen good little human. It's too dangerous and not worth the risk. I am here to protect you."

"Are you serious?" Nicole frowned. "Here I am offering myself and you're turning me down. What was all that 'I'm starved' and looking at me like I was your favorite dessert?"

"I'm not turning anything down...just taking a rain check." He leaned down to kiss her, but his lips landed on her ear when she turned her head.

"I don't give rain checks," her pride huffed as she tried to walk away. "And I don't like to be teased." Especially when she wanted him so damn bad.

He grabbed her arm pulling her back against the wall. "I wasn't teasing you." His eyes roamed down her body, "I love looking at you."

Nicole rolled her eyes with a snort, and then decided she could tease a little herself. "I guess I'll go take a nice long hot bath." Heat flared in his eyes and her belly tickled. He let her go, stepping back. "Help yourself to anything in the fridge since you're starved," she tossed over her shoulder.

Walking slowly into her room, she smiled. Ha...suck on that vamp. Grabbing her shortest shorts and a cut off tank, she headed to the bathroom. Running the hot water, she stripped out of her clothes making sure the door was cracked open just a tiny bit. Yeah, she was evil and proud of it. The way he was looking at her earlier had made her want him so badly and then he turned all big and bad protector on her. Yeah, well, two could play the tease game, so she made sure she walked back and forth in front of the cracked door as many times as she could...naked.

"Hey, could you put me a beer glass in the freezer to frost it up," she called out and grinned when he grunted his answer. Stepping into the hot bubbly water, Nicole gripped both sides slowly easing into it making sure she moaned her pleasure loudly as the water crept over her body. "Ahhhhh God...this feels sooo good," her husky voice echoed in the small bathroom flowing out into the rest of the apartment. At the sound of a glass hitting the kitchen floor, Nicole slapped her hand across her mouth giggling. She had never been one to play games or act the 'hoe' as Pam would call it, but this was certainly entertaining. Never had she considered herself a desirable woman. Men certainly hadn't been knocking down her door. The way Damon looked at her sometimes made her feel like the most beautiful woman in the world and it was an amazing feeling. "You okay?" she called out, hoping she sounded concerned. A loud bang followed by footsteps heading toward the bathroom sent her sitting straight up.

The bathroom door banged open with Damon's massive frame filling the doorway glaring at her, his eyes dark as they roamed over her sudsy body. Grabbing the bottom of his shirt, he pulled it over his head showing his sculptured body rippling as he threw his shirt behind him. Pulling first one gun out of the waistline of his jeans, and then one out of the holster strapped to his ankle above his boot, he placed one on the bathroom sink and the other on the toilet seat next to the tub never once taking his eyes off her. Kicking of his boots, he unsnapped his jeans and jerked them off showing that he was commando which was sexy as hell. He growled as Nicole's eyes focused on his arousal, something she didn't get to focus on the first time they were together. Her tongue snaked out licking her bottom lip wondering what he would taste like.

"I have never wanted anything, anyone, the way I want you," he growled as he stalked closer. "If we die tonight, it will be all on your head human."

Nicole pulled herself up to kneel, making room for him. "Yeah, but what a way to go," she sighed as he stepped into the warm water with her. As he sat, he gripped her waist lifting her to straddle him. "What was that loud bang?"

Taking his eyes off her breasts, he grinned up at her. "I put your bookcase in front of the door so I could have time to get my pants on if someone decided to plow through it."

Nicole's eyes widened before she giggled. "How sweet," she wiggled, getting more comfortable, feeling more female than she ever had in her life when he groaned his head falling back against the tub. Taking full advantage, she leaned into him kissing his jaw working her way to his neck. "I love the way you taste," she murmured against his skin as she licked her way down his neck to his chest taking a quick lick of his nipple. When he moaned, she went back and teased it with small bites before sucking it fully between her lips rubbing the pointy tip with her tongue.

Moaning deeply, Damon sat up leaning her back against his knees that were bent behind her since he was way too tall to stretch out fully in her tub. "My turn," he grabbed her hair forcing her head to lie back over his knees. Usually she hated having her hair pulled, but this was different and the dominance of it turned her on...wow, who knew she'd like being dominated. His large hands gripped her breasts pushing them together as his eyes devoured them.

"Not fair," Nicole's voice cracked with need. "I wasn't done tasting you."

As his head lowered to her breast, still pushed together by his large strong hands, he blew against one puckered nipple then the other. "Honey, if you tasted anymore of me, our bath time would be cut way too short." His tongue snaked out flicking across one nipple then the other.

Nicole moved, slowly rubbing friction against his hard cock that was nestled in the curve of her ass. As he feasted on her breast, his hands moved down her body to still her hips. This time, she growled with frustration. Reaching around, she grabbed his hair pulling him away sliding back onto her knees and before he knew what she was doing she reached under the water gripping him before she slammed onto him, sheathing him in her tight warmth.

"Ahhh...damn!" he yelled out, his fangs growing longer overlapping his lower lip. Leaning in she licked one cutting her tongue in the process of riding him hard. He grabbed the back of her head bringing their mouths together in a teeth crashing, tongue grinding duel and then stopped cold. "No!" his voice boomed in the tiny bathroom.

Too far gone with emotion, Nicole didn't see the change in his eyes or feel the stillness of his body, she just kept loving him toward satisfaction. Trying to lean into him to taste more, she realized he was not pulling her toward him, but holding her back...pushing her back. "What's wrong?" she whispered trying once again to lean toward him. "Damon?" His face had turned to stone and his eyes were a mixture of lust and something else she'd never seen before.

Looking away, he lifted her off him as he stood, jumping out of the tub. Grabbing a towel, he dried off quickly and pulled his jeans back on. "Are you still bleeding?" he asked, not looking at her.

"Ah, no," she replied confused. "It was just a little nick from your fang. Do you sharpen them babies?" she tried to tease as she got out of the tub. Grabbing the towel he threw on the floor, she wrapped it around her now chilled body.

"Get dressed," he demanded before storming out of the bathroom slamming the bathroom door shut behind him.

Staring at the door, Nicole felt her stomach flip, but for different reasons than before. This time it wasn't a good feeling. What the hell was that all about? Wasn't he a freakin vampire who loved blood? Or maybe it was her blood he didn't want, and dammit, that hurt more than it should and pissed her off which was a little demented.

Wrapping the towel tighter around herself, she opened the door and walked out. "What's the problem Damon?" Nicole walked in the middle of her living room noticing he was on the phone. She waited until he hung up. Standing there with her hands on her hips, she glared at him repeating her question.

"I need to go out for a while," he grabbed his bag shoving things into it, not meeting her eyes. "Jared is coming over to stay until I finish."

She walked closer putting her hand on his shoulder, and died a little inside when he flinched. "What did I do?" Nicole asked hating the pitiful voice that squeaked out of her mouth.

"Nothing, Nicole." He zipped his bag standing up straight not looking into her eyes, "You did nothing."

She had a sinking feeling that she knew what was up. She stepped into his line of vision forcing him to look at her. "Damon, I'm going to ask one more time what's wrong. I'm not going to beg, but I know something just happened and it's only fair for you to tell me."

His head turned toward her, but his eyes were slower to make it to her and when they did, she gasped. They were blacker than she had ever seen them and rimmed with fiery red. "It's not you Nicole. I just have to leave for a bit."

"You need to feed." Her hand flew to her mouth, "My blood did this to you?"

He nodded. "It's fine Nicole. I just waited too long."

Reaching up, she touched his cheek, "Then feed from me."

He stepped away from her as if her touch burned him. "No," his eyes shifted everywhere but back to her.

"Why not? I don't understand. I have blood...you need blood. You've helped me so much, let me help you." Nicole took a step toward him and he stepped back which was starting to piss her off a tad. "You act like you don't want me anywhere near you."

"I'm not taking your blood, Nicole," Damon hissed, taking another step back. "So just let it go."

"Why are you acting like this?" Nicole frowned.

"Like what?" he shifted glancing at his phone.

Okay, she wasn't an idiot and she could take a hint, like how he was shifting around wanting to get away from her. Yeah, been there done that. Well, she wasn't going to make it easy on him. Hell with that. "Like an asshole," she shot back. "Is my blood not good enough for you?"

"You don't know what you're talking about Nicole," he hissed, glaring at her this time instead of his phone.

"Then why don't you explain it to me. Do I even have a shot with you or am I the wrong species?" she snapped, closing the gap and poking him in the chest. "What is it vamp? I'm good enough to fuck, but not good enough to suck? What, my blood isn't good enough for you?"

He was silent, except for the grinding of his jaw.

His silence was enough answer for her. Even though her heart was trashed, she still had her pride that saw her through the worse moments in her life, and by God, it would get her through this. "You know Damon, I know all about vamps taking the blood of humans and the bloodlust, blah, blah, blah and I don't take it lightly, but *you* are a warrior and I trust *you* never to hurt me, but that isn't it, is it? You're afraid to be mated to a human. I know you can be mated to one because Jared told me."

"Jared's an idiot, but you're right. I don't want to be mated to anyone and I'll never turn you," Damon replied. "I shouldn't have let this go as far as it has."

"What, playing with the little human?" Nicole snorted. Walking toward the bookshelf he had placed in front of her door, she tried to push it out of the way, but it wouldn't budge. "Dammit..." She felt tears close and prayed to God they didn't spill over before she could get him out of the apartment.

"I wasn't playing with you," Damon marched over, moving her out of the way. She pulled her arm away from his grip with a snap. With ease, he picked up the bookcase with books and all, moving it back to where it was. He turned to look at her and for a brief moment sorrow filled his eyes, but then the emotion was gone in a flash.

"Just go, Damon," Nicole wished to God she had put her clothes on. She felt stupid standing in a towel trying to be all serious.

"You're the one with the friends with benefits idea," he snapped, then frowned shaking his head. "I'm sorry, I didn't mean that."

Wow, that was harsh and hurt like hell. With a sad smile, she cocked her head. "You meant it and you're right. I was wrong. I want more...you don't obviously." Sighing deeply, her heart breaking more than she ever imagined, she actually laughed with a bitter edge "You know, I thought it would be easier the older I got." She grabbed his bag handing it to him as she edged him toward the door.

"What?" Damon looked confused.

"Loving someone and having it thrown back in my face." Shaking her head before he could speak, she started closing the door, "I can't just have a one sided thing Damon. You have your reasons for wanting to stay distant and I understand, even though you won't talk to me about it, but I understand. The friends with benefits was because I wanted you so badly, and I hoped that you could find a way to love me."

Damon stuck his foot between the door and the frame before she could shut it. "You love me?"

"Yeah, Damon." Being honest was the only way she was going to know how he felt and she was sick of the back and forth stuff. Either he would stay and work things out, or he would walk away. It was in his court now, but the not knowing was going to end now. "I think it's obvious to everyone but you. I have never offered anyone else my blood, which by the way freaks me out, but yeah, I would give every ounce of blood I have in my body, for you. If that's not love, then I don't know what is."

They both stood still as stone, him in the hall and her holding so tightly to the door, she was surprised the wood didn't splinter. They stood staring at each other. As the minutes went by, so did Nicole's control. Finally, he moved his hand up to rub it down his face as if frustrated, "I don't know what to say."

"Well, that pretty much says it all." Nicole moved quickly before he could see the pain she was trying so hard to hide, "Goodbye Damon." The sound of the door snapping closed and the lock clicking, echoing through the room, hit her hard. Slapping a hand over her mouth, knowing Damon's keen hearing, she rushed to her bedroom closing the door quickly before grabbing a pillow to cover her face. Never had she felt this type of devastation. Not once had her love being turned down felt this way. Curling up, she lay down and cried into her pillow praying she was strong enough to survive the pain this time, truly terrified she wasn't.

Chapter 14

Pam flipped through the papers Nicole had finished, "Bored much?"

"You don't even know," Nicole snorted. "There's only so much I can do around here. My apartment has never been this clean...ever. Please tell me you talked them into letting me come back."

"Mitch is working on it." Tossing the paperwork on her briefcase, Pam sat at the kitchen bar. "At least they are letting you do paperwork here."

"Nothing has happened," Nicole flipped her hands up in frustration. "Seriously Pam, I think this whole thing was a bunch of crap. I mean, I don't even need around the clock bodyguards anymore."

"I believe that's because you refused their services, so they could use their talents looking for the ones responsible for all of this, so you could 'get back to your job'," Pam replied in one breath flipping her fingers up doing air quotations.

Rolling her eyes, Nicole took a bite out of the sandwich Pam brought her. "Well, it's true. The children are suffering, not me. The more warriors they have working on this the better."

"And, there she is again, Mother Teresa in the flesh." Plopping a chip into her mouth Pam grinned, "You never cease to amaze me."

"Whatever, Pam. You take your job as seriously as I do."

"They think Chad's missing," Pam laid that bombshell out.

"What?" Nicole sputtered, water dribbling out the corner of her mouth.

"He never came in to pick up his last paycheck or clean out his desk. Mitch just thought he was pissed, but then the police came by saying the neighbor's had called because his mail was overflowing the mailbox and newspapers were all over his driveway. No one has seen him since the night at the hospital." Pam twirled her phone around on the counter, deep in thought, "They think it's all connected. The attempts on your life, Mitch's and now Chad."

"So that means I'm still out of work," Nicole grimaced at how shallow that sounded. She and Chad had issues, but that didn't mean she wanted to see anything terrible happen to him.

"It doesn't look promising."

"That's so unfair. I mean all of you are taking a chance, so what makes me so special?" Nicole hissed, slamming her hand on the table.

"Honestly," Pam cocked an eyebrow, "we, as in all of us, are not sleeping with one of the highly acclaimed warriors."

Totally taken back, Nicole was speechless for a minute, "Excuse me?"

"Oh, yeah," Pam nodded. "I got the scoop from Mitch."

"Spill it friend. What scoop?" Nicole knew for a fact she was not going to like this one bit.

"That Damon told Mitch if you weren't pulled off the job, he would have the Council pull all the warriors out." Pam shook her head, "I just found this out today when I talked to Mitch about you coming back to work."

"That son of a bitch," Nicole yelled, stomping around the kitchen looking for something to throw. Picking up a glass, she threw it into the sink. She had never felt more betrayed in her life. He knew how much her job meant to her and to have it taken away because of him.

"Ahhh...Nicole you're bleeding," Pam got up to get a wet paper towel.

Swiping her cheek with her shaking hand, she saw the blood which ticked her off more because memories from a month ago when

Damon had refused her blood came back slamming into her mind. "Where is he?"

"Who Mitch?" Pam handed her the towel.

"No, that no good, blood suckin vamp." Nicole grabbed her purse heading for the door, "You coming?"

"Are you freakin kidding? I wouldn't miss this for the world." Pam grabbed her stuff and hurried out the door.

***

Nicole, with Pam following closely, slammed into the warehouse looking around.

"What the hell happened to your face Callahan?" Mitch bellowed stomping her way.

Okay, that was definitely a case of deja vu taking her back a step. Out of the corner of her eye, she could see Pam shaking her head at Mitch in warning. "Not now Mitch. I'll get to you later."

Jared walked up to them at that moment. "Everything okay?" his eyes went to each of them before landing on Nicole.

"No, everything is not okay," Nicole frowned. "Where is he?"

"Who?" Jared crossed his arms, his stance spread wide.

She went to go past him to find Damon herself, done with the games, but he blocked her path. "I'll tell him you're here and if he wants to see you, then he will," Jared glared down at her.

"Did you know?" Nicole felt her chin quiver and bit her lip hoping to stop it.

Jared just stared at her for a minute then nodded. She knew her mind was so wide open, he could probably read what she had for lunch a week ago. "Yeah, I did know, we all agreed that it was the best for you."

Closing her eyes, she dropped her head, "How could he do that to me?"

"He was trying to keep you safe," Jared shook his head. "Is your job more important than your own life?"

"My job is my life," she brought her eyes back to his, not answering his question directly. "It wasn't his decision to make."

"I disagree," Jared replied, his gaze softening a bit. "As your protector, he had every right. You can't save the world, Nicole."

"I'm not trying to save the world," Nicole lashed back turning and heading toward the door. "Just the ones that can't save themselves."

"I'll see what I can do to get you back on." Mitch told her as she passed. "If they pull out, then they pull out."

"You bet your ass you will Mitch, or I swear I'll go to a different county." Nicole pushed open the door walking into the night. She really didn't know what in the hell she wanted anymore. This whole thing had turned her world upside down and she didn't know what to do, what to think or who to trust. Pam followed her out.

"Nicole...wait," Pam ran up beside her.

Nicole stopped in front of Pam's car. "I don't know what to think anymore Pam. I mean, I don't want some pity party. I just want my life back. It wasn't the greatest, but it was mine. I know I'm anal about that, but I can't help it."

"I understand," Pam nodded and she truly did because she knew Nicole better than anyone. "I also understand their need to protect. I have learned a lot since working with Jared and I really think you need to talk to Damon."

Shaking her head, Nicole snorted, "No." She headed toward the passenger side of the car, but before she could open the door, she heard the door lock click. Looking up, she saw Pam holding the key lock.

"Do you realize since that night you haven't said his name?" Pam crossed her arms. "Jared said Damon's not doing any better than you are since that night. And do you know that he sits outside your apartment every night watching to make sure you're safe and if he can't, he makes sure someone else does?"

Nicole glanced up, eyes wide in shock.

"Come on Nicole. Do you really think that after all they have done, Damon would just say, 'Oh, okay, well see ya around' and leave you without protection," Pam rolled her eyes.

"I didn't think..." Nicole shook her head. God what a freakin mess. "I told him that I didn't need their protection...that I didn't want their protection."

"Why? Because he didn't want your blood?" Pam shook her head, "You know Nicole, I love you like a sister, but I really think you're wrong. I told you your heart was going to be in this for the long haul and dammit, I was right. You love him and to protect yourself, you pushed him away without even finding out why he refused your blood."

"I don't love him..." the lie stuck in her throat, "anymore."

"And once again, I call bullshit," Pam pointed at her. "You know I never figured you for a coward. You were probably the bravest person I have ever met, but now I don't see that in you at all. All I see is a woman who is letting others dictate her life and all you can do is yell and be pissed. Why don't you help yourself like you have a hundred times in the past and talk to him?"

Okay, that was harsh, but Nicole figured well deserved. "Yeah, well guess that won't happen since Jared won't tell me where he is."

"He's right behind you leaning on his bike. He must have been on watch detail and followed us here," Pam giggled at the horrid look that crossed Nicole's face.

"Are you serious?" Nicole paled.

"As a heart attack," Pam grinned. "And he's looking at you like he could gobble you up."

"I'm gonna kick your ass," Nicole grunted then turned around.

"Yeah, get in line chick." Pam unlocked her car and got in to wait, a wicked grin stretched across her face.

Nicole charged across the parking lot ready to let loose on the vamp, but slowed when she caught site of Damon, "You look like hell."

That half grin that she loved so much curved his lips, "You look beautiful as always."

Okay, that was a new one. He'd never complimented her like that before and it turned her brain to mush sending all kinds of girly feelings through her body. A small sigh escaped her lips before she straightened her spine. Dammit...get a grip girl. You don't need what's left of your heart stomped on. "Why did you do it Damon?"

He didn't even hesitate before answering, "To keep you safe."

"I'm not the only person doing this job," she countered, trying her best not to step toward him, wanting so badly to touch him and have him hold her. It had been such a hard month trying to get over this man and now seeing him so close brought it all back, like a punch to the stomach.

"You're the only one targeted."

His voice was strong and sure while hers was shaking and crackly...the jerk. Didn't anything about her affect him. "Not true. Mitch was targeted." Then added. "What about Chad missing. That could be related."

"He went after Mitch because he wanted to get to you. As for Chad, we don't know yet." Damon sighed, "Listen Nicole, we have been through this again and again. I did what I had to do for you and nothing more. You haven't been fired and you'll be back to doing what you love as soon as we catch this bastard."

Nicole rolled her eyes then turned to walk away, "Yeah, well hurry the hell up. I want to get back to work." Well, that was a train wreck. "And I didn't ask for you to do anything for me."

"I can't mate with you Nicole," Damon replied, his voice hard and firm.

Nicole stopped, but didn't turn around. Closing her eyes tightly, she held as much hurt back as she could. "And you're reminding me of this again because...?"

"I miss you," his answer was low, but loud enough for her to hear.

Turning around, she took a step closer, her head tilted slightly. "You miss me?"

He straightened from the bike taking a step closer, "Yeah, I do."

No, Nicole screamed inside her head. Don't do it girl. "Well...I miss you too," she whispered. "But I can't be with someone who can't be honest with me and trust me to share certain things. I know you won't take my blood or mate with me or turn me. What I don't know is why. And I can't live with that. You know all about my life, but I know nothing of yours. I want to know everything about the man I love, be able to share everything with him good or bad and well, I can't compromise on that. I'm just not made that way."

Damon was silent long enough that Nicole almost turned to leave, but he cleared his throat, "The first moment I saw you walk into the gym, I had an overwhelming need to protect you. Nothing else but protecting you matters, and I *will* go to any extremes to achieve it," Damon's eyes turned dark. "You were my total focus and I couldn't stop thinking about you. We react that way when we find our mate."

Nicole's eyes widened, but she kept silent not wanting him to stop.

"If I take your blood Nicole, you *would* be my mate," he took a step forward.

"And why is that a bad thing, Damon?" Nicole could not understand.

"Because I killed the last human who was to be my mate," his eyes never left hers. "I never had the feelings for her that I have for you, but I still wanted to be mated with her and was determined to do so."

Nicole frowned, embarrassed by the fact she was jealous of a dead woman. "How did you kill her Damon?"

"I was a young vampire then and didn't have control. She offered her blood to me and once I started, I went into a frenzy and couldn't stop. The next thing I knew I was holding her as her eyes stared up at me in horror." Damon finally looked away from her. "Her last breath whispered my name."

"My God," Nicole walked up to him wrapping him in her arms. "I'm so sorry Damon."

Damon held her close for a moment before gently holding her away. "I can't live through that again Nicole and with you, the draw is strong, so much stronger. I would rather die a thousand deaths than ever hurt you." Damon tipped her chin up so he could look deeply into her eyes, "I just wanted to let you know that this has nothing to do with you. It's all me and I wish things could be different because if there was any woman I would be honored to be mated to, it would be you Nicole."

Nicole locked her knees so she wouldn't melt on the parking lot. Was it possible for a heart to break twice so soon? A tear leaked its way out, rolling slowly down her check, but was stopped by his rough thumb before it could drip from her chin. "But it could be different," she voiced her hope out loud.

Shaking his head sadly, he took a step back. "It's not a chance I'm willing to take." When he saw her start to talk again, he put a finger to her lips. "Ever."

Nicole bit her lip to stop from begging him. Lifting her hand up touching his cheek, "If you ever change your mind you know where I am." Then she lifted up onto her tiptoes, and whispered close to his ear, "I have confidence that you would never hurt me....*ever*." She turned away, her heart in her throat.

Chapter 15

Pam didn't question anything as they quietly rode back to Nicole's apartment; Nicole was thankful. Her mind kept replaying Damon's words over and over again. She had never heard him talk so much at one time, and that he opened up to her, surprised her even more. Given time, she knew she could change his mind to take a chance on them. If he truly felt so strongly toward her, she had no doubt.

"Wasn't Damon on his bike?" Pam asked, her voice laced with concern, her eyes fixed on the rear view mirror. It was dark out and suddenly bright lights filled the car as Nicole turned to look out the back window.

"That's not Damon," Nicole screamed before the car rammed into them. The seatbelt saved Nicole from hitting the dashboard.

Pam fought to control the car as they were rammed again. "Oh God, hold on!" The car swerved dangerously out of control. The next hit sent them off the road down an embankment. Pam tried to get back on the road, but it was no use; the car hit something sending them flipping twice before slamming upside down against a tree.

Nicole opened her eyes slowly to find herself hanging upside down. The reality hit her foggy brain as soon as the pain did. "Pam!" Nicole called out as she struggled with her seatbelt. No answer sent her struggling harder, but her seatbelt was stuck. Using her hand, she pushed up off the roof of the car, lessening her body weight while the other hand frantically tried to unclasp the seatbelt. "Pam, please answer me."

Becoming light headed, Nicole spotted her purse and reached for it hoping to find something sharp to cut herself out. Something wet dribbled down her face into her hair. She knew she was hurt, but she had to get to Pam. "Dammit." Spots started dancing in front of her eyes as her stomach pitched with a sickening lurch. Not able to reach her purse, her body fell slack. She would try again in a minute. Trying to look around, she caught a glimpse of Pam hanging, her face turned away, but she saw blood, lots of blood. "Oh God...Pam!" Nicole screamed.

Nicole had no idea how long they had been there hanging, but it felt like forever. Thinking she heard someone outside the car, she had called out, but no one came. No one answered. She wondered where Damon was and why he hadn't come. Yeah, now she wanted his help. Ha...what a joke. God she was an idiot. She had tried to reach over to Pam, but couldn't reach. "Pam," Nicole's raspy voice cried, "Please wake up."

Thinking she heard footsteps, Nicole tried again to get out of the seatbelt, screaming, hoping someone would hear. Heavy footsteps came closer. "Please help!" Nicole called out. The car started to rock. Nicole screamed trying to reach Pam. She didn't care who was out there. She just wanted to get to Pam. She knew it wasn't Damon because he would have said something by now. Finally, the rocking stopped, the creaking of the car sounding eerie.

Hearing Pam moan, Nicole pushed herself up to look at her battered friend, but before she could do anything, her door was ripped from the car. Nicole screamed as a terrifying face appeared before her.

"Surprise!" Chad's chuckle was evil. "Paybacks a bitch...ain't it?"

Nicole swallowed hard. "Chad you need to help her." Nicole would beg if she had to. "Call 911. She's hurt bad." Nicole knew she was hurt also. She couldn't feel anything other than pain in her left ankle and her vision was blurring, so she figured that she probably had a head injury.

"Not gonna happen Nicole," Chad's speech sounded funny and she could see what looked like drool hanging in threads off his chin. "The bitch is as good as dead, and so are you, but not until we have us a little fun."

Chad snatched the seatbelt and with one strong tug it broke. Crying out, Nicole tried to brace herself, but it was no use; the momentum sent her falling on herself. Chad's hands grabbed for her. Trying to dig her way deeper into the car, Nicole realized there was nowhere to go. Fiery pain gripped her scalp as Chad clutched a fist full of hair dragging her out into the night and through the woods not caring that she screamed.

The louder she was the better because he had plans this night and it included Damon DeMasters watching his bitch die. He made sure not to kill the bastard before following Nicole, just delay him a bit until he was ready for his revenge.

***

Nicole woke up slumped on the floor of a small dank room. The smell of mold and mildew tickled her nose making her want to sneeze. Confused, she looked around slowly, her neck protesting in pain. God, her whole body felt like it was on fire. Movement from across the room made her gasp and then it all came back to her. "Where are we?" Nicole looked at Chad as she sat up straighter, her flight instincts taking over, sending the pain to the back of her mind.

"We, my lovely pain in the ass, are in your hell." Chad wiped his chin with his arm. "As soon as that bastard gets here, it's all going to be over."

"You're crazy," Nicole spat trying to hide her fear. Something was way different with Chad. "He *will* kill you."

Knocking the chair back as he stood, he rushed across the room so fast her eyes could hardly track him. "I don't think so." Chad knelt down flashing a set of fangs. "Now we are on equal playing field."

Nicole shrank back in fear, "What have you done?"

"What I should have done a long time ago." Chad grabbed her chin in a bruising grasp, "Do you have any idea how much money you have cost me?"

Nicole didn't answer. She couldn't take her eyes off his fangs. They looked too large for his mouth and drool kept leaking out the sides dribbling down his chin.

"No..." He forcibly shook her head back and forth answering for her. Flinging her face away, he stood and walked to the only window in the room. With his back to her, he stared out the window allowing Nicole to look for an escape...weapon....hope, but finding none, she focused back on him. "You are the cause of all of this. If you would have minded your own business and stayed out of mine, everything would have been fine. But no, you had to be little Ms. Perfect and save the world."

Realization flickered across her face. "You were setting up people to adopt vampire children to sell their blood," Nicole whispered sickened at the thought. "You used your job for your own greed. That was you in Stevie's house that night. You killed his parents."

Chad turned to glare at her. "It wasn't supposed to happen that way. We had an agreement, but then they decided they didn't need the money we could make on the vamps blood."

"So you killed them?" Nicole gasped in disbelief. She never really liked Chad, but never did she think he would have done something like this. Nicole pushed herself up shakily trying to stand, but her left foot couldn't hold any weight. She had seen a sharp piece of scrap metal lying next to her which she swiped before she stood. It wasn't much, but it was something. Leaning against the wall for support, she stuck the metal in her back pocket.

"It was you at the charity game," Nicole looked at him in horror. "You were going to kill Mitch."

"Never liked the son of the bitch anyway. People need to stop screwing with me," Chad sneered. "Just like you're about to find out."

"Did you put the hit out on me?" Nicole figured she might as well find out all she could.

"You were costing me money." Chad had to swipe at the drool again. "I owed some people, and every time I turned around, you were

164

taking kids out of homes I needed them in."

"That was you in the basement when I found Sam." Everything was making perfect sense.

"Right again," Chad sneered. "You have been a true pain in my ass, Nicole. Then those warriors come into the mix and screwed things up even more. God, I've been waiting for this for a long time, and I'm going to enjoy every bloody minute of it."

"Who did you owe money to?" Nicole figured the more she kept him talking the longer she could stay alive.

Chad laughed, "You really think you're going to put a stop to Crimson Rush don't you Nicole?" Turning from the window, he grinned with a shake of his head. "Well, I hate to tell you this Ms. Perfect, but you will be dead before the next sunrise, so looks like you failed all those kids you've tried to protect."

"The warriors are going to find you Chad," Nicole taunted. "You don't stand a chance with them."

"Oh, I got an Ace up my sleeve," Chad chuckled, looking back out the window.

"And what's that?" Nicole started to edge toward him sliding her hand toward her back pocket.

He turned, his eyes glowing red, "You, Nicole."

Chapter 16

Jared grabbed his gloves and slid them on, "Are you sure it was Chad?"

Damon lay on the ground, his bike lying a few feet away in pieces. "Yeah, I'm sure." Damon gritted his teeth. God, silver burned like a son of a bitch. "The bastard took me out and before I could get my senses together, he threw these damn silver chains on me." Silver didn't burn through clothes, but any skin it hit kept them immobile. Damon didn't know why or how the hell it worked, but he hated the stuff with a passion.

Jared pulled the chain from around Damon's neck. "That's gonna leave a mark."

"Hurry the hell up," Damon growled. "I don't know how long I've lain here. He could have Nicole and Pam by now."

"Who do you think changed him?" Jared pulled the last of the chains away and watched Damon jump up, wobbling slightly, then pull himself together. "Don't know and don't care at the moment." Damon took off running in the direction the women headed, Jared hot on his tail. Anyone driving by wouldn't have even seen them, their speed too fast to track.

Duncan met up with them as soon as they found the wreckage. Jared ran to Pam. Testing for a pulse, he looked over at Duncan, "She's alive." He tried to wake her, but she wouldn't wake up which probably for the best. She had some major injuries and needed emergency treatment. "Call 911."

Damon checked the other side of the car, but knew he wouldn't find her. Opening his senses, he closed his eyes feeling with his mind. He could smell her fear and helplessness. He had to get his rage under control in order to help her. One thing for sure, he was going to kill the son of a bitch. Turning his head toward the wooded area, he walked that way noticing a trail of flattened ground. It was as if

166

someone had been dragged, breaking through the grass and weeds.

Duncan came down the hill. "Go with him," he told Jared. "I'll stay with Pam."

Jared nodded, then headed in the direction Damon had taken.

Not going far, they stopped just inside a wooded area. A small shed type structure sagged in the clearing. A light glowed from a window outlining the shadow of a man. Damon made a move toward the structure, but Jared stopped him, "Hold on there, friend. He isn't strong enough to sense us, but you go in there with him standing right at the window, he can get to her before you get to him."

Damon knew he was right, so he forced himself to stop. "As soon as he moves, I'm in." His eyes never left the window. "You go around and see if there's another way in. As soon as you hear all hell break loose, get in there."

"On it," Jared slapped him on the back.

Damon took a quick glance his way. "Can you get a read on her?"

Jared sometimes forgot Damon couldn't. "Yeah," he nodded. "She's hurt, but okay. She's scared and is praying that you find her."

Damon nodded, looking back at the window, the gleam in his eye more determined. He heard Jared take off and waited, giving him enough time to search around to find another way in. The window Damon planned to go through wasn't large, but he'd take out the whole side of the building to get to Nicole. He could break through the door, but the bastard would be expecting that and Damon always did the unexpected, which was probably why he'd been around for hundreds of years. Nothing was going to stop him.

He could hear the river lapping the banks downhill from where he stood. The place looked like a good wind would knock it over. Yeah, nothing would keep him from her. Nothing.

Teresa Gabelman

Nicole shivered, her fear overtaking everything she felt at the moment. The adrenalin pumping through her body helped her pain. She wanted Damon to find her so badly, but she was afraid for him. She didn't want him hurt because of her. Too many people's lives had been disrupted. Looking around again for something other than the piece of metal in her pocket, Nicole noticed something. A rope was tied to the door that stretched to the ceiling where the end of the rope tied onto a curved hook. Understanding shifted the floor beneath her feet. If Damon came through that door, he would be impaled.

"I see you noticed my handiwork," Chad's laugh was evil. "Took me a while, but it works like a charm.

Suddenly angry, Nicole took a stumbling step toward him. "Damon is too smart to fall for that. If it does hit him, it will just piss him off."

"Well, that's where you're wrong. I had it coated in silver. Cost me a pretty penny, but every cent was worth it just to see that bastard die as the silver spreads through his body." Chad slobbered more as a wide smile spread across his grotesque mouth, "Oh yeah, worth every last cent."

She was not going to let him kill Damon. "You know Chad you really are stupid," Nicole spat, then chuckled, hoping to make him mad enough to come closer to her. Just close enough she could use the piece of metal in her back pocket. She wasn't sure how to kill a vampire, but she was sure a piece of metal, silver or not, through the heart would be a good start. "Damon is way smarter than you. He's going to kill you, do you know that? You don't stand a chance against him or any of the warriors for that matter. Damon is more man than you could ever hope to be."

Chad's eyes glowed redder as he turned away from the window taking a step toward her. "We'll see about that bitch," Chad snarled, spittle shooting out of his mouth.

"Yeah, whatever Chad," Nicole snorted, knowing her 'whatever attitude' would piss him off; it always had before. "All I know is that when Damon and the warriors show up, and they will show up, you're dead."

"Shut up!" Chad roared, his eyes going wild. "Just shut the fuck up."

Nicole's fake giggle worked like a charm. Seeing him move in her direction, her hand moved to her pocket, but before she could reach it, the window Chad had been standing in front of, exploded with glass, wood and one huge vampire. Damon blasted into the room, his arm hooked Chad taking him to the ground rolling away from Nicole.

Screaming, Nicole shielded her face and turned away from flying glass; she then watched in horror as the two fought. Damon grabbed Chad throwing him against one wall and then another, stalking after him pounding him in the face, so full of rage he could barely contain it. Never had Nicole seen him so angry. He again threw Chad against the wall before looking at her. His eyes calming slightly as they stared at each other. A click of a gun broke the silence as well as their eye contact.

Chad stood against the wall pointing a gun at Damon with one hand while the other felt for his fangs. "You bastard," he probed at one broken fang. "You're going to die."

"Now that's just gonna piss him off," Jared sighed shaking his head then thumbed over his shoulder. "And your crude looking torture thing didn't work."

"God, I hate you warriors. You think you're so fucking great, but I got you assholes now," Chad grinned, his broken fang dangling.

Jared rolled his eyes shaking his head. "I know you're new to this vampire stuff, but what you learn in becoming a vampire 101 is that bullets won't kill us."

"But silver ones will," Chad sneered with an evil grin that caused his broken fang to fall off. The ping of it hitting the floor was the only sound in the room.

Nicole saw the look of surprise on Jared's face, then she looked at

Damon who was staring at her with such sadness and loss, it took her breath away. "No!" Nicole started forward, dragging her injured foot behind her.

"I'm sorry Nicole," Damon gave a small sad smile. "Once he takes me out, kill the bastard," he ordered Jared, his eyes turning cold as he focused on Chad.

Frantic, Nicole felt the metal piece cutting into her hand, her grip white knuckle tight. Looking down, she saw a small thin stream of blood coming from her fist. Remembering Damon talking to them during one of their training sessions, she turned her other wrist over staring at it. A new vampire could not resist the scent and sight of fresh blood being spilled. It drove them into a frenzy, so it was very important not to get cut or have an injury near a newborn vamp. Looking up at Chad whose eyes were wild, his breathing panting, she knew he was on edge now and spilled blood may give Damon and Jared a chance to stop him.

Everything from there seemed to happen in slow motion. Always one to hate pain and blood, Nicole surprisingly didn't even hesitate putting the sharp metal against her wrist. With a small prayer, she took a step forward.

"Chad." Nicole was surprised her voice was strong and clear. Lifting her arm toward him, Nicole sliced her wrist open to the bone, hoping it would spill enough blood fast enough to make Chad lose control. "You lose."

The last thing she remembered was seeing Chad rush her, but before she was hit, he was taken down. She was caught before hitting the floor. Damon's face wavered in front of hers, his eyes worried. "I got you." Damon laid her gently on the floor. "God Nicole, what were you thinking?" Damon whipped his shirt off, wrapped it around her wrist and applied pressure.

"Saving you." She wanted so badly to reach up and touch his face, but a weakness so heavy settled over her body.

Damon looked away from her for a second. When he looked back at her, a lone tear of blood streaked from the corner of his eye down his cheek. "Stay with me, Nicole." His voice sounded so far away.

Nicole choked, and then struggled for breath. Oh, God she really didn't want to die. "I'm scared."

"You're going to be fine Nicole. Just hold on for me darlin." Damon put more pressure on her wrist trying to stop the flow of blood, but it just kept flowing. His fangs had grown large and long at the sweet scent of her life spilling on the dirty floor. "Fuck," Damon hissed under his breath.

"No, I'm not," Nicole whispered. She felt so tired and cold. Her eyes closed slowly and then opened, her vision blurry. She wanted so badly to ask him to save her, to turn her, but she wouldn't. She loved him enough not to beg him to do something he was so against. "Damon, please stop and listen to me."

"Nicole-" Damon pressed harder.

"Please, Damon," her voice cracked, growing weaker by the second. Knotting his shirt tightly around her wrist, he picked her up in his arms cradling her head softly. "Promise me something," she finally said after licking her dry lips.

"Anything darlin-" Damon's voice also cracked with emotion.

"I like when you call me that." Nicole gave him a small grin, her eyes closing. Clearing her throat, she leaned closer to him. "Promise me you won't give up until you've caught whoever is behind Crimson Rush. Take care of the kids for me."

Damon stayed silent as he rocked her back and forth kissing her forehead. He felt Jared at his back and knew Chad had been taken care of. He wondered if Jared had kept him alive so they could get names from him, but his only concern right now lay in his arms dying, and he knew time was running out. He had never met anyone like her ever. Instead of begging to be changed so she could live, she wanted a promise from him to take care of others. He knew she wouldn't ask for herself because it wasn't in her to do so, and also she knew his feelings on it and respected them. "I promise darlin," he whispered lowering her to ground gently. "I promise." But Nicole was beyond hearing.

Chapter 17

Nicole didn't know how long she had fought her way out of the darkness and pain that had devoured her mind and body, if this was the way to heaven, then a lot of people were gonna be so disappointed cause it sure wasn't fun or peaceful. Her heavy eyes fluttered open to slits. Afraid to open them fully, she moved her eyeballs only to see darkness. Wasn't there supposed to be a bright light to greet her? At least the pain was gone. Feeling a little braver, she opened her eyes more, and was shocked to find she was in a room, obviously lying on a soft bed. Nicole sat straight up looking down at her wrist which was free of any scar. My God, how long had she been out or was she really dead and this really was heaven.

Whipping the covers back, she jumped out of bed amazed at how great she felt. "Hello?" she called out, her voice strong and deep. Okay...she was starting to freak a little. God, she was thirsty. Licking her lips, she felt a prick of pain on her tongue. "Ouch." Reaching up she touched her lip, bringing her hand back she saw blood and her stomach clinched tight with hunger.

Eyes wide, she ran to a mirror hanging on the wall between two windows and bared her teeth. Short fangs hung slightly lower than her other teeth, sharp and pointy. Slapping her hand across her mouth, she turned away from the mirror. "Oh. My. God," she murmured behind her hand. "He did it." Turning back around, she removed her hand, slowly baring her teeth again. So many emotions sent her body into overdrive making her feel ill.

After flashing her fangs this way and that, trying them on for size so to speak, Nicole walked back to the edge of the bed and plopped down, stunned. She was a vampire, a freaking vamp and she had no clue how to feel about that. A little scared...yeah. A little freaked...hell yeah. What did this mean? Where was Damon and where was she? Whose room was she in? As if summoned by her questions and thoughts, the door opened and in walked Damon looking handsome and strong. She wanted to run to him, but his expression stopped her.

"What are you doing out of bed?" Damon demanded, his eyes running down her body back to her face.

"Why?" she whispered, ignoring his question with one of her own.

Damon was silent for a long minute staring at her so intently that Nicole shifted nervously on the bed. "I had no choice," he finally moved, setting the tray down on a dresser.

Okay, so that wasn't the answer she wanted. "Yeah, you did," her chin lifted in a stubborn tilt. "You could have let me die."

A frown spread across his wide mouth, "You need to feed."

Okay, that took her back and made her pale. "Feed?" Nicole hadn't thought about that. "Blood?"

His frown turned up a bit. "Yes...blood. You have been out for three weeks. I actually expected you to be out longer."

"Holy crap!" Nicole shot up from the bed. "Three weeks. My turtles. My rent is due. Oh my God. I have to get out of here." When she started to head toward a bundle of clean clothes lying on a chair in the corner of the room, pain clenched her stomach tightly causing her to bend over. "Ouch." Nicole's panicked eyes flew to Damon's.

"You need to slow down Nicole." Damon was next to her in a flash. "You're still weak and you need to feed."

"Ugh...will you stop calling it that," Nicole cringed. "It makes me sound like an animal or something, no offense."

Damon actually chuckled, "None taken." He led her back to the bed. "Your body has been through one hell of a change and will take time to adjust. We kept you in a semi-coma after the change, so your body could get used to the blood and you wouldn't suffer as much."

Sitting down slowly, she wrapped her arms around her stomach dreading the next pain. "But I feel great except for this."

"You will feel great. No aches, colds, headaches or disease, but when hunger hits, it's ten times worse than human hunger and the only thing that can satisfy it is blood."

"Yummy," Nicole rolled her eyes with a grimace.

Damon looked away from her. "Are you sorry I changed you?"

Shocked, Nicole realized he was nervous about her reaction to being a vampire. "I won't lie, it freaks me out a bit and yeah, I'm a little scared, but I'm still here. You saved me Damon and for that I'm grateful." She shrugged her shoulders, "I mean, you'll help me won't you?"

Giving a short nod, Damon poured some blood in a cup. "Here, you need to drink this."

"Why am I taking a cup? Don't you guys suck each other?" Nicole repeated what she'd thought in her head. Okay, that didn't sound good. Geez, this was going to take some getting used to.

Damon's eyes turned a shade darker. "We take our blood from a live source yes, but we do not suck each other."

"You know what I mean. Sorry, I haven't started the vampire 101 class yet." Nicole took the cup peering in it. Sticking her finger into the thick red liquid, she brought it to her nose and sniffed, then touched it with the tip of her tongue. Oh God, she was not going to be able to do this.

"What the hell are you doing?" Damon sighed shaking his head.

"Listen vamp, this is my first time taking some blood, okay, so chill out," Nicole shot back. A frightening thought crossed her mind, "Where did this blood come from?"

"What does it matter?" Damon walked toward her. "You need to drink it, Nicole."

Shaking her head, she tried to hand it back to him. "Thanks, but no." She felt another pang of what she now knew was hunger, but ignored it. "Maybe later."

"Nicole, you *are* going to drink it, so stop messing around or I *will* put you back into a coma until you are well fed and your body is adjusted," Damon growled.

Knowing he wasn't kidding, since he didn't seem to have a freaking sense of humor at the moment, Nicole brought the cup to her lips. Closing her eyes, she pinched her nose with her other hand and took a sip.

Damon smiled at her antics of pinching her nose. "What the hell are you doing now?"

"It's what I did when I was little and had to take medicine that tasted yucky." Nicole wiped her mouth with the back of her hand with a grimace. "Ugh...it's cold."

"If you wouldn't have taken forever to drink, it would have been warm." Damon rolled his eyes, but damn she was cute. Her little fangs peeking out from her upper lip was sexy as hell. "Finish," he ordered.

Nicole gave him an evil look before tipping the cup all the way back and downed it, nose pinched closed. Handing him the cup, she wiped her mouth again shaking her head. "That was..." Eyes popping open in horror, she grabbed her stomach. Looking around, she saw a garbage can across the room and ran for it. Just as she reached it, her body heaved, spewing the blood back out of her body. Damon was there holding her forehead as her body rid every drop of blood she had just drank.

"Easy darlin," Damon eased her back so she could sit down, then he went to get her a wet cloth. When he came back, Nicole had her head in her hands, her shoulders shaking. He knelt down beside her. "Hey, what's this?" He tilted her face up with both hands catching the tears with his thumb.

"I can't do this Damon," Nicole hiccupped as more tears fell. God, she hated crying. "Some vampire I'll make. I can't even stomach what I need to live on. The only thing I can really live on," she jerked away from him, and stood on shaky legs.

"Did I just hear you say you couldn't do something?" Damon teased, trying to get her back on track. An emotional, slash hungry new vampire was a ticking time bomb.

"Yeah, you did," Nicole frowned, and wiped her eyes looking in the mirror at her blood streaked face. Even knowing vampires cried blood, the sight of it running down her pale face caused her to fold into herself and slide to the floor. "Oh God, you should have just let me die."

Damon reached down picking her up into his arms before sitting on the bed. He cradled her close. "I couldn't."

Nicole sniffed peeking up at him. "Why Damon? I know how you felt about changing me."

"I couldn't lose you Nicole. There was no thought to it." Damon held her tightly, and then hooked a finger under her chin lifting her face closer to his. "And while we are on the subject, if you ever, and I mean *ever*, do something like you did by hurting yourself, I will blister that cute little ass. You got it?"

"Well, I couldn't lose you either, so I did what I had to do," Nicole argued her point then decided to take a chance - again. "I love you, Damon."

Damon closed his eyes tightly, and when they opened ,they were brimming. "And I love you, my little vamp." He bent to kiss her, but she pulled away.

"Really?" she looked shocked, yet endearingly hopeful.

"As you know, I'm not a man of many words, so when I do say something, I mean it," Damon growled. "Now if you'll agree, I think it's time I made you my mate. My blood will sustain you, be enough for you, when we are mated."

Happiness like she had never known before zinged through her body. She straddled him more than willing to take his blood if it would mean they would be together forever. Her love for this vampire so great. Suddenly, a horrible thought crashed into her mind. She pushed him away. "Oh my God, Pam!" Nicole struggled to get away. In all of this, she had forgotten about Pam.

"Is fine and will be fine," Damon growled grabbing for Nicole. "You know, I fell in love with you the first time I watched you put others before your needs. I have never seen anything like it. But now, it's just pissing me off."

"She's really okay?" Nicole leaned a little closer.

"Yes, she really is," Damon sighed, reaching up kissing her neck as he ran his fangs along the side of her neck. His hands were doing some roaming of their own. "If you really want to see her, we can go and take care of us later." He finished that statement with his tongue demanding entrance into her soft mouth.

Nicole was so lost in the kiss, she kept following as he pulled away. Nicole pushed him back down. She would call Pam first thing in the morning. Hell, they might not ever make it out of this room. Now that she had him, she didn't want to share.

A loud knocking broke their silence. "Damon, everything okay?" Jared's voice came through the door loud and strong.

"I am going to kill him," Damon groaned. "We're not leaving this room until you're my mate."

Nicole giggled at the pained expression on Damon's face when Jared knocked again. Then both Nicole and Damon looked toward the door shouting, "Go away!" Damon added, "Don't come back!"

Jared laughed from the other side of the door, "Glad to have you back Nicole," Jared called out. "If you need anything...anything at all, just let me know. My blood is yours if you need it. Glad to have ya in the vamp family babe."

Damon sat up grabbing the lamp off the table next to the bed and threw it. Nicole watched in horror as it splintered into a million pieces. "Go the fuck away Jared," Damon roared glaring at the door. "And if you ever offer my mate your blood again, I will kill you, slowly."

"Well hell, congrats," Jared hollered back, a smile in his voice. "It's about time, cause I was about ready to steal her away from your slow dumb ass." Jared's footsteps stomped away from the door.

"I'm really going to kill him," Damon rubbed his eyes lying back on the bed.

Nicole laughed and kissed his cheek, "No one can steal me away from you ever. So let's make this official before someone else comes by."

Damon growled as he pulled her under him. "Thank you," he peered down into her eyes.

"For what?" Nicole was confused.

"For loving me," Damon looked slightly embarrassed at his own words.

"You're welcome vamp," Nicole smiled, nuzzling his neck. "Oh, and you owe another dollar to the jar."